Chester County Fiction

Edited by

Sue Gregson

Christine Yurick

Oermead Press

CONTENTS

Foreword   v

NICOLE VALENTINE – *The Weeping Beech*   1

ROBB CADIGAN – *Baptism*   10

JIM BRESLIN – *Real Gentlemen*   24

JOAN HILL – *The Acceptance Letter*   34

VIRGINIA BEARDS – *A Hunt Tea*   47

Fall Out and Frock Coats   52

No Good Deed…   58

RONALD D. GILES – *The Prey*   65

CHRISTINE YURICK – *Sam's Brother*   79

JACOB ASHER MICHAEL – *As Clouds Will Always Do*   85

PETER CUNNIFFE – *An Incident Near Paoli*   93

WAYNE A. CONAWAY – *Formerly Fearsome*   113

Fit For A King   116

TERRY HEYMAN – *The Ocean's Breath*   119

MICHAEL DOLAN – *The River Runs Red*   139

ELI SILBERMAN – *The Great Neck Nazi Killer*   155

Contributors' Notes   187

FOREWORD

If you live in Chester County, PA, you have probably visited Iron Hill or Victory Brewing Company. Each restaurant offers beer samplers, where diners can sip a variety of beers—ales, ports, stouts, and lagers—and determine which best suits their palate.

Although this book is considered a short story collection, I believe the reader should approach this book as a sampler. The stories here were not chosen from a slush pile of submissions based on one editor's preferences. Instead, I reached out to local fiction writers I admire and asked if they would contribute. The writers in this collection have varied backgrounds. One holds a doctorate, several have been previously published, others are working on their MFA or have attended writers' retreats. All understand the most important part of writing is to keep one's "ass in the chair." These are writers that I'm proud to call friends, and I'm thrilled each of them has agreed to collaborate.

Inspired by the weeping beech tree in West Chester, Nicole Valentine crafted a story of magical realism that takes us back in time. Robb Cadigan offers a reflective piece about a man seeking redemption as he tries to find his way home. Ron Giles provides a drama where the hunter becomes the hunted. Peter Cunniffe shows how a contemporary high school scuffle mirrors the escalating violence of the Revolutionary War. Christine Yurick felt the urge to write after a recent tragic event made national headlines. Joan Hill and Terry Heyman both offer stories of women in transition. Michael Dolan's story will haunt those who fish and canoe along the Brandywine River. Jake Michael reminds us that the most important gift we have is to live in the present moment.

A few humorous stories balance out our sampler. Virginia Beards offers a fun triptych that explores the lively characters who fox hunt in southern Chester County. Wayne Conaway contributes two comic pieces that he often reads aloud locally.

Eli Silberman has been working on an intriguing novella about seeking revenge over the passage of time. We're fortunate he has given us a sneak preview with this adapted short story.

Each of the writers who contributed to this sampler has their own unique voice. Our editors, Sue Gregson and Christine Yurick, worked with each writer to polish their stories, to draw out their visions. Be sure to check out our contributors' notes at the end of the book for both a bio and a note on the origin of each story.

I also have to profusely thank the artists who pulled together the cover. Graphic designer Larry Geiger's brilliant designs have made a mark on the West Chester Story Slam and now in this cover design. Photographer David James took a series of stellar photographs, making it difficult to choose just one. It's been great fun to work with these creative professionals.

Writing is a solitary activity, but we are lucky in this day and age to have ample opportunities for writers and artists to meet and share their passions. Whether it is the Brandywine Valley Writers Group, local readings in coffeehouses, or meeting for a beer at the Story Slam, writers and storytellers from throughout our region are able to connect, coach and converse, cheer each other on.

In all, there are sixteen stories here from thirteen writers, neighbors of yours, who are dedicated to their craft and inspired by this bountiful place in which we live. We hope you enjoy this sampling of local writers and find a few that suit your taste. Enjoy!

Jim Breslin

Chester County Fiction

NICOLE VALENTINE

The Weeping Beech

At the end of a weedy alley, behind an ugly chain link fence, lives a 300 year old weeping beech tree. Signs point the way for intrepid naturalists, or history buffs, who take the time to find it. If it's not the middle of summer, when the tree is hidden by a curtain of leaves, you'll be able to peek through the fence and see its massive gnarled branches spreading out in all directions. This mammoth tree has survived three centuries of storms, drought, flood, pollution and the relentless progress of man. It takes a reader's curious mind to stand there and wonder how and why this specimen has survived so long. This is the story the tree whispered to me one winter afternoon.

I didn't lead the most exemplary life. This is true. I was your classic cad with a square-set jaw and youthful swagger, and I used my God-given gifts to further my own goals. The early eighteenth century was a different time, you see. Your County of Chester was a very different place. I did not have the "moderne conveniences" you all enjoy, and when left with the option of starving or committing a few minor sins, my conscience quickly stepped aside and gave way to my gut. So, yes--I stole, I lied, and I preyed on dim-witted innocents. Still, I challenge anyone reading this to say that I, Nathaniel James Bowdoin deserved to be trapped inside a

1

tree. Not just any tree either, a Weeping Beech that has had the distinct misfortune to have lived now for over 300 years.

There is no greater sentence I have ever heard of, three centuries of wooden imprisonment for a few minor transgressions. Yes, Merlin was trapped forever in his Hawthorn tree, but that dear friends, is just a myth.

I am, quite sadly, very real.

I should've known not to make the acquaintance of anyone named Bane. Alexander and Mordecai Bane, brothers and neighbors owning two large portions of what you now call East and West Goshen, and both in possession of lovely wives neither of them deserved — but I digress.

Mordecai was the eldest, though by no means the bravest. He let his fool of a brother pave the way to Pennsylvania and once he proved it could be safely done he followed. They came from Scotland, enjoying that generous land grant from William Penn himself. I had followed soon after from my home in France, believing that perhaps the stories were true and the colonies were everything God had promised, and then some. The Banes were Quakers and good honest men — the worst kind really. There is no reasoning with good, gentle people.

I set up my own existence at a small tavern run by a portly old Frenchman named Cayley and his rather friendly, much younger wife, Auda. She wasn't a great beauty, but the knowing look she would give me as she passed me on the stairs each morning led me to find her far more attractive as each day passed. I knew it was inhospitable of me to partake of Cayley's young femme, but he was a Frenchman. I believed, as a fellow countryman, that if he had discovered us the whole incident would've blown over rather quickly. I was wrong.

It was Cayley who introduced me to Alexander and Mordecai. Cayley sealed my fate, and for this I should hate him; but, I suppose I've already taken my pound of flesh from Auda.

It was a sweltering day in late August when it all began. I had my morning romp at the tavern with Auda and then

promptly set out to meet Cayley at
Bane. I was looking for land, an
plenty; three hundred acres each.
and was hoping I could take advan
knew my motives, he made no mention
was holding out on receiving some sort of
brokering the transaction. He proceeded to in
with the same deference he'd bestow on a member of
nobility. I removed my toque and shook Mordecai's han
first.

"It is with great pleasure that I cross your threshold this
morn. I have heard kind and judicious words in description
of both you and your brother. You have been described as
eminent country gentlemen," I said, bowing low and deep. I
looked up to discern whether my manners were eliciting the
correct response.

"I have no more resolved in my mind whether I am
qualified for such a description than for that of King or Sul-
tan," said Alexander. I could not tell whether he was
mocking me or himself.

Mordecai remained silent.

I proceeded to walk around the small farmhouse ex-
claiming it to be the finest establishment I had seen since my
arrival to the colonies.

Mordecai finally spoke with a cryptic line that I imagine
was a quote from some infernal book of manners.

"Be no Flatterer, neither Play with any that delights not
to be Play'd Withal."

While he spoke those words, a wisp of a girl entered the
room. I had never in my life witnessed such unadorned perfection. She had the complexion of fresh cream; a high color
of natural pink in her dewy cheeks and hair so blond it held
onto the very rays of sun. It was nearly the color of spun
sugar; translucent and glowing with a light all its own. It
formed a halo around her exquisite features; adding a pow-
dered wig, or even a mere dot of rouge, would have been a
blasphemous act punishable by the very angels of God. I

peak nor move in her presence. She was the most
uman specimen of beauty I'd ever lain eyes upon.

rprised to find anyone else in the room, she cast ceru-
eyes up at me for only a moment, before lowering them
urely back to the floor and whispering a shy apology.
e had seen me, I was sure of it.

I was given only a few seconds to observe her, but I
drank her in with such intensity it was if I had spent hours
studying that face. I engraved her upon my conscience and
found myself wishing that she wore the low, sweeping neck-
line so fashionable among the French nobility. I would
spend the next few weeks obsessing over an expanse of skin
I witnessed only in my mind. For days afterward I dreamt of
nothing but trailing the pads of my fingertips along a valley
of purest white, only to watch it flush pink beneath my
touch. I imagined her sighs of pleasure and could not bear
the thought of any other man being the first to elicit them. It
had to be me.

My imprisonment had begun.

Her father, Mordecai, ushered her out of the room with
some excuse that her morning Bible studies were yet to be
finished. I watched her depart with great sorrow and realized all eyes in the room were now on me. I promptly closed
my mouth and regained my gentlemanly composure, eras-
ing any traces of lust, but the damage was already done. I
had made the fatal error of not controlling my emotions fast
enough.

"That is my daughter, Hannah," Mordecai growled. This
was no mere explanation. It was a declaration. My. Mine.

Any civility that was in the room was now gone, and
knowing it would not return I made gentlemanly remarks
and quickly excused myself.

I left the Bane homestead with Cayley desperately trying to keep up with my gait, yapping in my ear about other
men with large land grants who might sell, but I paid him
no attention. I was too busy trying to figure out how I'd
make my latest acquisition of virgin land. I had to have
Hannah.

I left her alone entirely for two weeks. I had a feeling that Mordecai would be watching her closely, as fathers often do with daughters that age. I don't want you to think I was in the habit of deflowering young girls. Frankly, it had never been an interest of mine. I preferred the company of whores and married women. Women who knew their way around a man's body; women I knew could please me. Yet, something about Hannah held my fascination. I could do nothing with my time other than figure out how to get closer to her, to make her mine.

Her days were made up of staying very close to home so getting her alone proved a useless endeavor. The only chance I had was attending a Quaker meeting. I had to show an interest in God and see whether I would be welcome into their society. This would prove difficult. Their sect had seen imprisonment and torture only several decades prior and generational memory can be very strong. Add to the fact that I had apparently garnered a terrible reputation for being untrustworthy and my presence wasn't exactly applauded.

However, a large tenant of their belief was that all humans have the light within them, and they had to admit that even I was human. They welcomed me to attend, and there I could furtively sneak glances as Hannah walked in and out of the women's meeting room. I have no idea what they discussed in that refuge but in the men's meeting there was entirely too much talk of eradicating slavery. I found myself bored; but I stayed the course and feigned interest.

I made a big show of acting incredulous, and then letting them slowly sway me. I discussed the merits of abolition, and I agreed that allowing slavery to exist would mean we would have to agree it was possible that men could come steal us away to strange countries for the same purpose (in truth, I found this a ridiculous concept as I always had my pistol constantly by my side).

Every time I saw Hannah pass I made sure my gaze was focused on her. I willed it to be a weight so heavy she would stumble under its gravity and turn to see where it came from.

One fateful day, she finally did. She turned back and recognized me, and the high color returned to those pale cheeks and my heart and cock leapt at once. She looked at me. She saw me. I was now determined to make sure she would think of me as often as I thought of her. I would make sure I became her obsession as well.

In time, I had bought the affections of most of the elders. I began to make myself more and more useful to the congregation, volunteering my efforts when necessary. All the while, I felt Mordecai's glare heavy on my own back. He ran interference as much as possible, keeping Hannah far from me. He was civil enough, and I'm not sure if he was buying my metamorphosis or not. Either way, he certainly did not think I was worthy of his progeny.

My luck finally returned to me in early October. I was able to find Hannah alone for a few seconds. It was then I made a very risky gambit. I took her hand in mine and as she attempted to pull it away I held fast. I looked deep into her eyes and pressed a letter into her palm.

My dearest Hannah,

I can do nothing but think of you day and night. I yearn to speak with you; to see your smile and know it is meant for me. Will you please take pity on me and meet me in your woods Tuesday afternoon? I hold you in the highest regards dear girl, and I wish only to tell you, how your mere existence has changed me for the better.

Your servant,
Nathaniel

This could have gone very wrong. She could have, and rightly should have, taken the letter immediately to her father. I would have been cast out, and lost all hope of ever seeing her again. Miraculously, the very next day, she presented me with a reply by dropping a small blue paper in the dirt as she walked by. I nearly ran like a schoolboy to fetch it. I was so thrilled that she deigned to respond.

Nathaniel,
I will see you. I will come before supper, and I can only stay a
moment.
Hannah

It wasn't much for my hopes to ride on, though it was something. She was already disobeying her father in communicating with me; I had hopes that this behavior would continue.

I studied her handwriting carefully that night. It was miniature; tendrils and spikes rooted themselves low and peaked high; dancing loops and undulating arcs balanced perfectly. In all its complexities, the words still existed in a simple straight line.

I dreamt her words were tattooed down the side of my torso..."I will see you. I will see you." I became obsessed with being seen.

I remained at Cayley's tavern, but cut off all relations with Auda. I was focused on my one object of desire, and I could not bear to delight in another until I had conquered her. Auda seemed quite put out at first by my change in behavior, but I believed she attributed it to my new found religion and let me be. I did not tell her about my intentions with Hannah; this was my secret alone.

But, women are always far smarter than they let on, and Auda found my correspondence to Hannah. In a fit of jealousy, she told Cayley that I had taken advantage of her. I was truly wrong about him being a typical Frenchman. Things did not blow over as I had predicted. Cayley headed to Bane's woods that evening, waiting for me with a loaded musket.

Can I blame him? I wronged him; I truly did. I can't say I've ever been in the position to love someone and have her belong all to me, to only have her taken away. I suppose if I had, if I could've been with Hannah—perhaps I would've reacted similarly. I believe I would've done anything to keep her, to be near her.

I left for the wood, no idea how dire my situation would become. With every dusty footstep along the road I feared the worst. Not Cayley. I had no idea he lie in wait. I was petrified of Hannah. What would lie in her beautiful face? Would it be full of reproach? Would she tell me I was too far from God? My very being hung on what I would read in her features.

Crows flew overhead casting shadows along the dirt below and cawing warnings that I could not understand with my human ears.

Only now, with my veins coursing with sap instead of blood, do I remember them as, "turn back, death awaits."

Hannah was there before me waiting, and I realized as soon as she stepped toward me that in all my machinations to own her, to control her — I had completely lost control of myself. She was smiling, even her eyes were lit with a light that told me she loved me. I was, all at once, whole. She believed me to be a good man and at that moment I believed I could be. I could be anything she wanted me to be. Her smile was all I needed for the rest of my life.

If only the rest of my life continued from there.

The musket boomed and I felt nothing but the fall. I hit the hard earth and felt the wind escape from what was left of my lungs. I heard Hannah scream, and I felt her hands grab mine. She was crying, and I was being swallowed, further and further into the soil, into the cold earth. She was the last thing my human senses registered. The very last words that vibrated through my ears were "I love you. Please, please don't leave me."

I decided to fight. I would not continue to sink into the clay and dirt. I would claw my way back to my body and Hannah. I could not possibly leave this life now that I had been truly seen. Hannah knew me like no one else ever would. I clawed, and I scraped my way through soil and root, desperately trying to make my way back into a body that would no longer have me. It was then I believe the tree decided it would take me.

Perhaps, it took pity on me. Perhaps, I was headed for a place far worse and it knew that. Whatever its reasoning it pulled me up through its wooden soul. I felt myself being tunneled through a vast root system, and I thought of Hannah's writing, her loops and tendrils and I let myself ride them like intricate veins to what I hoped was her heart.

And here I am still. I watched her live and grow to an old woman. I watched them bury her in the family plot when she died. While she yet lived, it wasn't that bad. She would come and sit under my branches and think of me. She would often talk to me; the way people do at the graves of those they've loved. She never knew I was sheltering her with my boughs, that my leaves whispered to her in the wind.

She could not hear me. I could no longer be seen. Here I have sat in my wooden prison and mourned her for years. I've watched her children, and then her grandchildren, grow old and die. I've watched the Earth turn on its axis so many times I've lost count. One day maybe the heavens will deem me saved, and declare I have paid for all my transgressions. Then I will see her smile again, and I will know that I've been seen once more.

ROBB CADIGAN

Baptism

"It's me."

The laundromat payphone is the first phone you've seen for miles. The receiver, slimy with years of sweat and neglect, sticks to your palm. You try not to think about it. Remnants of a "Re-elect Rendell" bumper sticker cover the number pad in sun-washed red, white, and blue. You only need the zero.

"I know who it is. The operator said your name. That's still how it works. You ain't been gone that long."

"Yeah, well, thanks for accepting the charges."

A snort. "What, they teach you some gratitude in that place? That one of the steps?"

An old woman in a housecoat is sorting her laundry on the machine closest to the phone. She makes no effort to hide her eavesdropping. You apparently are her source of morning entertainment, probably the first good show she's seen all week. Ten times better than "Wheel of Fortune." You switch the phone to the other ear, turn your back to the woman, and try to think of what to say next.

"Listen, I need—" No, that isn't right. "Look, I'm coming to see you. And I was wondering if, do you think maybe I could get a ride?"

Slow response, like a person waking. Labored breathing, the tobacco wheeze still front and center.

"I know you don't like driving no more," you say. "I wouldn't call if I didn't ... I don't know. I didn't really plan this out. It's all right if you can't. I'll be fine."

You wait. Listen to more breathing, more wheezing. The sound of a lighter igniting, an old song you will hear in your grave.

"Where are you?"

You look through the front window at the traffic on the entrance ramp to the bypass. The cars are crawling west, toward the Lancaster outlets. Too damn hot to go shopping, but that's what people do. Nothing else here. You can't remember which ramp it is.

"Excuse me, ma'am." The old woman starts, as though you suddenly ripped the phone off the wall and hurled it over her head. "Where am I?"

She takes a step back, afraid. She looks you up and down, lingers on the long hair, the sweat-soaked t-shirt, the jeans no one in his right mind would wear on a day as hot as this. Maybe she should be afraid of you.

Suddenly, the woman raises her hand and waves, like you're some insect bothering her while she is trying to watch a parade. You sneer, but let her brush you away.

"I don't know where the hell I am," you say into the phone.

The reply, obvious but no less cutting, comes only after another long pause.

"Some things don't change then."

You let the bait float there on the surface. Just like they taught you, drilled into you every damn day. The world outside is endless temptation, words and gestures in grand conspiracy to drag you down again. Life must be played as a game of defense. That's what the counselor said anyway. You're not sure you believe that, but you remain on guard just the same.

"Look, it's hot and I'm tired from walking."

"You couldn't have been walking that far. You'd be here by now."

"An hour, something like that."

"An hour? An hour'd put you near what? — Downingtown, probably. Hell, that's a nothing walk, day like today. Do you good."

"It's gotta be a hundred degrees--"

"Not here. Your mother's been blasting the AC all damn morning. It's like Ice Station Zebra in here. But you know us, made of money. I'm just sitting here waiting for the Phillies and watching my dollar bills float by on the nice cool br--"

"Forget it. I'll walk."

Another break, another pause.

"Look, you been gone a long time."

"A month, give or take."

"That's not what I'm talking about. You been gone a hell of a lot longer than that. Let me tell you something, all right? You listen to me now. Don't be surprised if people ain't in no hurry to take you back, and don't go feeling sorry for yourself about it all. That's just how it is sometimes. How it should be after all you done."

"All I've done?" You stop, count backward, another thing they taught you. You're trying your best, but you can feel the ground eroding beneath your feet and you know you don't have long before it all gives way. "Right. I get it."

"I'm just sayin'. Not everybody's gonna be all happy for you."

"Like you?"

Another breath, the longest yet, plays out at the other end of the line. "I took your call."

"Yeah, I know. Like I said, thanks for that."

You wonder what Frankie would do right now. Frankie always knew how to handle this crap. Frankie didn't hesitate, didn't worry about consequences.

"So, can you come get me or not?"

"I think I already answered that."

"You want me to walk?"

"Here's how it is. My door is open. It hasn't been and now it is. You want to come home, then you can find your way back. The way I see it, that's sort of the whole point."

"You don't think I'll make it."

"I ain't given it all that much thought one way or another."

Like hell.

"I'll be there."

"I guess I'll see you then."

And there it is, glistening along the edges of your father's voice like fresh blood. Doubt. They warned you to expect it, to be ready for it. You told yourself you could handle it, told yourself it wouldn't bother you.

You hang up the phone without saying anything more. It bothers you. But you keep walking.

Truth is, you don't mind the walking all that much, even in this heat. People around here, they don't know what real heat is. A thermostat gets reset after years of patrols in foreign deserts. Deserts with names you will never pronounce right, deserts you will never scrub from the cracks in your skin, as much as you try.

No, you don't mind the walking, but you sure as hell wish you were flying again. Life was all so much easier when you could fly. Never worried about where you were going. Just flying, away from wherever you were.

Frankie used to say there was nothing to it. Just lean back and let the wind lift you into its arms like you were a newborn baby. All innocence and belief. Sure, there was that split second when fear and thrill intertwined and you felt yourself lose control, but Frankie said that was normal, that was where the real fun was. Just surrender to it, he would say, give in. So you would. And when you did, you were a planet, a star, your worries as small as your comrades far below.

Frankie and you in the clouds, brothers in arms.

But today you're walking.

The bypass isn't made for walking, not really. No shade, for one thing, which makes the blacktop that much hotter. The shoulder is wide enough, but the cars zoom by so quickly you feel the rumble of them pass too close with every step and it makes it hard to turn your back. You hate to turn your back. Every once in awhile you do face the traffic with your thumb stuck out, but you know the gesture is nothing but empty hope. Nobody will stop, not for a guy like you. Thirty days away don't change a man all that much.

"Can I help you, son?"

Son. The cop actually says this.

The cruiser has pulled onto the shoulder, blocking your path. Two cops remain inside, too lazy or too hot to bother to get out of the car. The officer on the passenger side motions you over. You can only stare back at him, your image a funhouse reflection in his aviator sunglasses.

"What's the matter? Don't you talk?"

You wipe the sweat from your eyebrows. This doesn't help. "I talk."

"Good. That's good." All neck, and muscle gone to flab, the cop rests his thick forearm on the doorframe. A skinny, younger version sits behind the steering wheel. He never looks away from the windshield, but instead just keeps staring at the stretch of Route 30 rolling out ahead.

"So, what I'm asking," the cop says, "is whether you need some kind of help. Hot as hell out here. I'm thinking maybe a guy shouldn't be walking, you know, in weather like this."

"I'm not doing anything. Just walking."

The cop's eyes sweep over you, the duffel bag, the boots. "Just walking. All right, uh huh. Where you walking to? Not out here for exercise, I wouldn't think."

Sweat runs down your back in separate streams, soaking the waistband of your jeans.

"I'm walking home. Is that a problem?" You've forgotten to count backwards, the way they taught you. "Lemme ask you something. You usually stop people from taking walks? Has some new law been passed I don't know about? I been away a little while, so maybe I missed it."

The cop smiles with phony patience. "I don't think you wanna do that, son."

"What's that?"

14

"I don't think you wanna be mouthing off like that, not today. Too hot to be talking like that today. Got me?"

He looks like he is about to say something else, but then sits back and folds his arms. He exchanges a look with his partner behind the wheel. The radio inside blurts a message, but you miss it.

"Where you been?" the cop finally asks.

"Been?"

"You said you were away. I'm asking you where you've been, because I'm looking at that artwork there ..." The cop points at the tattoo running over your deltoid, the eagle and the towers, wrapped in the flag.

You shift your stance, your boots feeling tight on your swollen feet. "I'm just out for a walk, is all. Heading home."

"I understand. But what I want to know is — "

"Why?"

"What's that?"

"Why d'you want to know?"

"I'm just wondering if you served, that's all."

You don't want to be like this. You don't like yourself this way. All you really want is to fly again, to take to the skies. You figured a month away would have stopped you from thinking about it — that was the promise, after all. But once you've flown so high, like a hawk, like a superhero, it's not so easy to let that go. Today you've thought about little else.

The cop considers you for a long minute. The radio brays its noise once more. The driver mutters something, but again it's too low to hear.

"Might be better to get off the bypass," the cop tells you. "Just do that for me, OK? It wouldn't be good to have to clean you up from the pavement here, know what I mean? Not after what you've been through. Wouldn't make no sense, going all that way and getting yourself killed when you come back home."

Home.

As the cruiser pulls away, the gravel spinning lightly beneath its tires, you close your eyes and wait for that breeze to find you, to carry you away. But nothing comes. And when you open your eyes, the haze in the distance rises from the pavement like the vapor of spilled gasoline.

When the next exit ramp finally appears, you decide to take the cop's advice and get off the bypass. You follow the ramp down to the access road, a little-used country lane. This part of the county remains undeveloped and likes it that way. Nothing around but an abandoned gas station and a bar, tucked into a clump of trees singed black by a forgotten fire.

To call the bar a dive would be charitable. The building itself is not much more than a concrete bunker, with a single window facing the street. A Yuengling sign hangs crooked against the glass, its faint neon buzzing like a warning.

As you open the door and step inside, a wave of air conditioning washes over you and you decide at once that you will never leave this place. You stand there by the door, basking in the chill, waiting for your eyes to adjust to the dim.

The room is as long and narrow as a bowling lane, with a tired brass-rail bar running the length of one side and a few tight booths tucked against the back wall. The place smells of cigarettes and stale beer and ghosts.

The kind of dive Frankie would have loved.

The bartender looks as though he's been there since the First Great War. Gray buzzcut, deep-set eyes, a welterweight's broken nose. He rubs a soiled white towel over wood that long ago lost its sheen and eyes you with an expression of suspicion mixed with annoyance.

"You need a shirt in here. We don't want no ... you need to wear your shirt."

There's no one else inside. Too early, maybe, although this doesn't seem like a place that lives by the clock. You'd think there'd be at least a couple guys off the graveyard shift or wrapping up an all-nighter or someone like that. But the place is empty.

You grab your t-shirt from your back pocket and pull it over your head. The bartender doesn't seem satisfied.

"Brutal out there," you say.

He gives you a whatcha-gonna-do shrug. "August in Philadelphia."

"I was looking for a drink."

"We're not open yet."

"The door was open."

"Shouldn't have been. We're not open yet."

Maybe you expected things to be different, but you haven't been away that long. The world didn't change overnight. Frankie always liked to say that, given the chance, people are assholes more often than not. The real nature of humans.

It wasn't like this when the towers fell. When the towers fell, people were climbing over themselves to help each other. In a matter of hours, the country went all Kumbaya. It was like a curtain peeled back on the world and we all got a glimpse of what could be, only to have the scene go dark again before we ever got a good look.

"Not open? All right, well, maybe we could work something out."

The immediate problem at hand is that you have no money, not one dollar. They give you bus fare when you leave, but only when you leave on their terms. Not when you just walk out. Tucked deep into your duffel, there's a Velcro wallet with one credit card inside, but you have no doubt she closed that account two seconds after she kicked you out.

"Listen, the thing is, I don't have any cash."

"That right?" Nothing more than that.

"Please, it's so damn hot outside. I just need a drink, anything. I'm happy to pay for it, more than happy, but like I said ... we'd have to work it out. Maybe I could send you some money when I get home? Maybe--"

The old man shakes his head, slowly, like it takes too much effort. "This look like a bank to you, son? You see a big vault back there, any—what do you call—tellers, yeah. You see any tellers here?"

The bartender finally stops moving the towel. He knows something is off, something isn't right. Probably sees it in your eyes. Crazy don't hide too well.

"I was only asking if--"

You're not crazy. Damaged, discarded, alone. You are all of that, but you're not crazy.

"Look, I don't want to deal with this right now," the bartender says. "I just got in, you know. I ain't got time for crap like this."

"Just a glass of ice water?"

Frankie would just take the goddamn drink. Hop over the bar, shove the old man out of the way, and help himself to whatever the hell he wanted. You, you're a slow burn. You can feel the embers inside you, still glowing, waiting. You feel the fire rising to your cheeks, through your hands. Your fingers fold into fists, your heartbeat rises. You feel it all, and you fight it back. Loosen those fists and fight it back.

"I'm sorry, I understand," you say, offering a small smile as peace. "Maybe I could ... d'you got a restroom I could use?"

"You should go."

"Please. I've been walking a long time. I'll be quick."

The old man rubs at the bar again, back and forth, back and forth, then finally shakes his head.

"I don't want a problem here. Too damn hot, too damn early, you know what I'm sayin'?"

He's saying what everybody else is saying. What they've been saying since you got back. That you don't belong, that you're not welcome.

Frankie told you it would all be no problem, but then Frankie was the eternal optimist. A thousand people can teach you how to fly, but there isn't a single one who will show how to land. That, it seems, you have to figure out for yourself. Your own return home was a spectacular crash and burn, a riot of disappointment and heartbreak. A disaster it will take years to recover from.

As you open the door, the heat wraps itself around you like the arms of the Devil himself and you sink into it, leaving the bartender scrubbing at his imaginary stains.

The payphone clinging to the post outside looks worse than the one in the laundromat. You don't expect it to work. And you definitely don't expect her to accept the charges. There is no reason for her to take your call. She says as much.

"I shouldn't be doing this. The court—"

Her voice sounds like honeysuckle, like daybreak after a good long sleep.

"The court isn't here. This is just you and me. Us."

"But the judge said we shouldn't ... that you can't—"

"Screw the judge."

You let her consider this, let her think it through. She always liked to think things through.

"I'm sorry," you finally say.

"Sorry?"

"I just wanted to hear your voice. It's been so long."

"This isn't right. I shouldn't be talking to you."

"I know, I know. But please, just for a minute—" Your voice catches, surprising you. "Talk to me."

"I don't know what to say—"

"Anything. It doesn't matter."

"This isn't a good idea. I should go."

"No. Please. Just talk to me."

When she sighs, you know you have her, at least for a time.

"Why don't *you* talk to me?" she finally says. "Tell me how you're doing."

"Good."

"No, I mean really."

You pause, searching. "Better. I'm doing better."

You met in high school. Whenever she told the story, she insisted it was in math class, but you thought it was at a dance. She was probably right. You didn't go to many dances. But you remember the first date. A movie—*Apollo*

13. She talked through the whole thing. Nerves, probably. You didn't really mind.

"How's work?"

"Busy. Jeff thinks the fall will be worse than last year."

Jeff.

"But Monica is leaving, so that opens up—you don't care about this."

"I do. Tell me. Monica is leaving, so..."

You try to remember Monica.

"So I might get moved into the supervisor job. I'm a candidate for it, at least. That's what Jeff says, anyway."

Jeff again. The guy at the Christmas party. One of those salesman types, with a double handshake and a bleached smile. A tool.

"That's great. You'd be perfect for that, you know."

You started living together right before the towers. She found a little house in Phoenixville, just off the park. The place needed a lot of work, but you were up to it. You even liked the work, the feeling of accomplishing something with your own hands. Most of all, you liked knowing she was happy. You had friends over for barbecues on the patio out back, walked into town to the bars and the restaurants, and talked all the time about the days when your kids would run around in the park.

Frankie, he had a girl back in Boston. Patty. He called her his little peppermint, which would have sounded stupid coming from anyone other than Frankie. Frankie never gave a shit how he sounded.

"Where are you?" she asks. "What's that noise?"

"Nothing. Just a truck going by."

"Truck? I thought you were calling from—"

"No, I'm out. Furloughed."

"Has it been a month?"

She knows it's been a month. She probably has it on the drugstore calendar on her refrigerator, your refrigerator, with big red Xs over each day.

"I'm doing OK. Honest. I just wanted you to know that." You draw a deep breath, trying to remember your script. "And I wanted to say, I wanted to tell you that I'm sorry. I never meant for any of this. I never meant to hurt you. That night, you gotta understand...shit. Just, everything's going to be OK, you know?"

In her silence, you can hear her apprehension. You struggle for words that will put her at ease.

She hadn't wanted you to enlist. Not that she didn't believe in the cause, but she wanted you home. There was a whole life she envisioned for you both and she didn't want that changed. Let someone else be a hero, she said. Let it be someone else's time.

You didn't listen.

"Look, I think I should go," she says.

You want her to stay, to hold on. Like she used to. You tell yourself you will never hurt her again. You tell yourself you will protect her, be there for her, love her. These are the words you shared in evening circle every day, the amends you wanted to make. But courage will take longer than you hoped.

"I understand."

"Where are you going to ... where will you live?"

"I'll be at my folks' soon. I only have a little more ways to walk."

"Walk?"

"I'll be fine. I'm almost there."

You can tell she wants to say more, so you wait. Somewhere to the west, a dog barks, the sound echoing around you like sniper fire.

"Good. That's good," she finally says. "Well, you take care of yourself, OK? I'm glad you're doing all right."

You ask if you can see her sometime. But when the phone goes dead, you realize that she has hung up and you try to convince yourself that she never heard your question at all.

You decide to head away from Lincoln Highway and instead follow the country road into the trees. Perhaps you can find a creek, cool water to drink. You seem to remember a crossroad not far north. You figure you can turn west when you reach it and maybe make your parents' place by late afternoon, in time for dinner.

But you walk for another hour, maybe more, and when the crossroad you remember never appears, you know that you are lost. Still, you move forward, because turning back seems pointless.

You no longer think of flying, but instead find yourself preoccupied by your thirst and the heat. Your vision is bleary and you worry that at any moment you may collapse here by the side of the road. As you come around yet another bend, the evergreens seem to sink away, revealing a new mirage, particularly cruel.

A farmhouse sits on a small plot of green land. The structure is not unlike the house you grew up in, although the roof slopes at a different angle and the clapboard siding is painted white, not the patriot blue your mother loves. A rocking chair sits empty in the shade of a covered porch.

On the front lawn a woman holds a garden hose, watering the flowerbed that stretches beneath a bay window. The plants bloom in a beautiful palette, colors you are certain you have never seen before.

Her back to the road, her attention to her chore, the woman does not see you.

Her hair is twisted into a bun beneath a white cap. She wears a black apron over a blue dress with long sleeves and you can only wonder at how uncomfortable she must be. But she doesn't seem bothered by the heat, not in the least.

She can't be real.

The Amish don't live here. On occasion, you would see them in their carriages, their horses keeping a slow pace along the shoulder of the road. But their homes are farther out, across the county line. You know you haven't walked that far, wandered that far off track.

Yet here she is.

The water spills from the hose as your salvation. A sip is all you need, a few swallows to wash this dryness from your mouth.

But you don't approach. You know you will frighten her if you step onto her lawn. Instead, you stand there on the road, your t-shirt tucked once again into the back pocket of your jeans, the duffel bag resting at your feet, your skin drenched with sweat.

Perhaps sensing you there, the woman finally turns. She is not frightened. She stands without moving for a time, considering this stranger who has come upon her, until she raises her hand. Raises her hand in what you take as a small wave.

You raise your own hand.

She beckons you onto her lawn.

You hesitate, because you always hesitate, but she waves again and pulls you over the property line.

The water flows, soaking the same spot in her garden, creating a pool in the mulch. The woman doesn't seem to notice. Instead, she watches you come to her. Your hair is matted, your face covered with dust and dirt, your posture bent by fatigue and shame.

Still she waves you closer.

You have no words. Instead, you point to the hose, to your own lips.

The woman nods, then, bestowing a smile like a gift, holds the hose toward you. You cup your hands beneath its stream, letting the water fill your palms until it overflows. Then, you drink.

At last, you drink.

Exhausted and overcome, you drop to your knees, sinking into the damp earth beneath you. You feel the life flowing back into you. You glance to the porch, where you see Frankie sitting in that chair, rocking back and forth, back and forth, with the same old smile on his face, his wound healed by a miracle.

As you close your eyes, the woman raises the hose above you, so that the cool water cascades over your scalp and neck, running in tributaries down your back, washing you clean.

Real Gentlemen

My friend Jack pulled off the highway onto the shoulder, slowing down on the gravel, before turning into a short, rutted driveway. We were picking up Lester, who lived with his old man in a little Cape Cod, just a little shack by the side of the highway. The dust kicked up as we pulled in behind a battered red pick-up truck. An ugly mustard-yellow refrigerator stood guard at the corner of the house, the fridge doors set to the side, leaning against peeling clapboard siding. Knee-high weeds surrounded the house and a swing set sat rusting away in the corner of the small yard.

Jack leaned on the horn. Through the car window, I watched the front screen door of the shack swing open hard and fast. Lester appeared just as the door slammed into the siding. He strutted down the two steps.

The screen door rebounded shut behind him and we heard a gruff voice yell something from inside. Lester raised his hand over his shoulder and stuck his middle finger straight up back toward the house, as if he was saluting not just his old man, but his whole lot in life.

He wore a white wrinkled dress shirt with the top button fastened over his bony frame. His black belt strapped tight around baggy faded jeans and he sported a pair of nicked up black dress shoes that hadn't been shined in years. But it was Lester's hair that struck us all.

"What'd you do to your sideburns?" Jack asked as

Lester climbed in the back seat next to me. Jack adjusted his rearview mirror to take a look.

"I trimmed them off. Sideburns are for commies."

"Dude, you look like a felon," Tony said as he twisted around in the passenger seat and stared wide-eyed at Lester.

"Turn the fuck around," Lester replied, shoving Tony in the back of the head. Lester turned to me in the backseat and chuckled.

Lester's sideburns had been shaved off, the hair above his ears cut straight out. His face was taut, with darting eyes and a hawkish nose and his cropped hair was short and tight. He fidgeted with his hands. Tony was right. I imagined we'd picked up a convict who'd just gotten out of the pen.

Jack, Tony and I had been friends since freshman year. But Lester was new to our crowd. One day the previous week when Jack picked me up to see a varsity basketball game, he stated, "We're giving Lester a ride," and that was it. Lester was in, but it didn't last long. I'd had figured out the other guys, but nobody ever figured Lester out.

We'd usually hang together on Friday and Saturday nights and cruise around. Eat at the local diner. Catch a movie. Sometimes there'd be a school dance or a party. Typical small-town excitement.

"What do you girls got planned tonight?" Lester asked with a sneer. He had this strange way of demeaning those he was with.

"I'm hungry. Let's eat. Did you eat?" Tony asked. Jack looked over his shoulder and saw the road was clear. He stomped on the gas and the tires screeched in the gravel until he'd pulled out onto Route 1.

"I'm thirsty," Lester announced. "Hey, Jack. Make a right, will you? I want to grab my stash." Jack turned right at the traffic light. On our left, the Brandywine Creek meandered alongside the winding road. Lester leaned forward, scouting ahead. "This is it," he glanced out the rear window as Jack slowed the car. "I'll just be a minute."

Lester hopped out and scuttled like a crab up the embankment into the woods on our right. Jack continually glanced in the rearview mirror to make sure a car wasn't sneaking up from behind. Lester reached around a tree and brought out a bottle, then scampered down and hopped back in the car.

"Go!" he said breathlessly as he shut the door.

"What have you got there, Lester?" Tony asked.

"A little Wild Turkey. If you're good, I may even share it with y'all." Lester unscrewed the lid and took a swig.

"Goes down smooth, boys," he announced before exhaling a deep breath.

We passed the amber bottle around, each taking a swig. Jack waved the bottle away since he was driving. I tilted the bottle and felt the warmth of the whiskey course through my chest. We cruised along with the Brandywine River on our left, the sun setting beyond the marshlands. The road followed alongside the water's path, and Jack took the road easy. We were in no hurry. We had no plans.

Eventually, Jack pulled the car into a gravel parking lot by some hiking trails. We sat in the car and passed the bottle around as the sun slowly dropped behind the hills. We talked about football, movies and girls.

"You getting hungry?" Tony asked again.

"It's still early," Jack said.

"We go there now, we'll have nothing to do all night."

"Let's go to Hank's Place," Tony repeated. "I'm freaking hungry."

"In a bit," Jack said. "We'll go in a bit. You guys in?" he asked over his shoulder.

"Sounds good."

As Jack and Tony talked up front, Lester sat silent next to me as though the liquor had aroused a sorrow in him. I smacked him in the shoulder in an attempt to bring him back around. "You up for Hank's Place?"

"Yeah, Hank's Place sounds good," Lester said. He was looking out at the fields, where a flock of geese was flying low, preparing to land in the field by the creek. I watched as they set their wings for the final approach and in my mind timed my shot as my father had taught me to when we hunted out near Parkesburg. "Take aim and shoot just as their wings set, son." I noticed Lester's hands fidgeting with the bottle.

"You okay?"

"Did you ever feel you got to fight for each fucking inch in your life?" Lester asked.

I just looked at him. His eyes were red. I wasn't sure if it was the whiskey or something else.

"Nah, you got it good," he said as he wiped his nose with the back of his hand. He looked out his window as he cradled the bottle on his lap. "Your parents are together, eh?" He asked.

"Yeah," I responded awkwardly.

"Sometimes you take what you can get," he said with a sigh. "It might not be what you're expecting, but it's okay all the same." He took another swig and handed me the half-empty bottle.

The greasy smell of burgers and fries smacked me as soon as we entered Hank's Place. We took a booth and looked around for a waitress.

"What'll you have, gentlemen?"

We ordered burgers and sat back in anticipation. The waitress brought our sodas. Jack poured salt on the table and started shaping intricate designs with his fingertips.

"What are we doing tonight?" Lester asked as he tapped on the table. "This cruising around is boring."

"I don't know. Anyone know of a party?" Tony asked.

"No."

"I don't."

"Wanna see a movie?" Jack asked.

"I don't want to see a damn movie." Lester unfolded a napkin and inserted a corner in between his shirt buttons making a bib. "This town is full of chumps." He picked up his knife and fork. "Let's shake things up." He thumped his fists on the table as he held the silverware. "Let's start a fight," he said, then a little louder, "Let's kick some ass!" The three of us stared at him.

"Dude, settle down," Jack said.

"Let's drive down to Maryland," Tony suggested. "I heard there's a strip club off Route 1 that we can get into."

"I ain't driving to Maryland," Jack replied. "My dad would kill me if we got caught down there." He shook his head. "Christ, that's all I need."

It looked as though we'd end up sitting in some parking lot, listening to the radio and dusting off the Wild Turkey. But then, in a flash, I glanced up and saw this gorgeous girl standing at our booth.

"Hi Tony," she said with a wide smile. "What's going on tonight?"

Tony introduced Jack, Lester and me to Shelby. She had auburn hair nicely tied back in a ponytail, big blue eyes and a flirtatious smile. Damn, that was a fine smile. She was dressed real sharp, wearing a tight green sweater. She had her act together, and I could tell she liked Tony.

"I'm just hanging with my friends." She pointed to a booth back in the corner. Three girls in the booth were eyeing us up and giggling. Shelby said, "We're going to hang out at my house tonight. You should come by for a little bit."

"Are your parents home?" Tony asked.

"Right now they are, but they're going to the Huffman's house for a party," she said. "You can come hang out, they won't be home until after eleven."

"We just might do that," Tony replied with a grin. "We just ordered, but we'll stop by when we're finished."

"Sounds good," Shelby said and spun around.

We all watched her walk back to the booth. When Tony turned back to us, he was beaming. "Well, boys. We've got some plans now!"

"What does she want with chumps like us?" Jack innocently asked.

"You're killing me," Tony scoffed.

"Where does she go to school?" I asked.

"Villa."

"Oh no, a private-school girl?"

"Don't worry. Shelby's cool," Tony said. "Her dad's a bit of a hard ass. He's some tough guy lawyer. But we'll stop in for a bit and then scram before he gets home."

Lester lit up next to me. I'd never seen the guy smile like that. The waitress brought out four plates with burgers. Tony, Jack and I started eating but Lester was giddy, as though he'd never been to a girl's house before.

"What's your problem?" I asked.

Lester shot me a look. "No problem." He grabbed the ketchup and spurted some on his fries as he tapped his foot under the table.

I glanced over at Tony, who just shook his head and sighed.

We ate quickly and silently. After counting out the bill and the tip, I hustled out to the car to get the front seat but Tony called "shotgun" on me. I was stuck in the back with Lester again. I climbed in. Lester slid the bottle out from underneath the front seat and took a prolonged swig.

"Let's get laid!" Lester said with a wicked laugh, then louder, "We're gonna get laid tonight!" He punched the back of the seat and laughed, "Yeah, baby!"

Jack spun around. "Lester, easy on my car."

My burger wasn't mixing well with the Wild Turkey. The thought of riding in the back with a hopped-up Lester was making me nauseous.

Jack headed out on the highway and Tony fed him directions. He turned onto a side road. After a ways, Tony said "I think this is it, yeah this is right," and Jack turned at an oversized black mailbox onto a long driveway with a white fence on either side.

"She lives up there?" Jack asked. "Whoa!"

Perched on the top of a hill, a classic white farmhouse was silhouetted against the night sky. The driveway crossed over a small bridge before curving up the hill. Off to the side sat a huge bank barn. Our headlights swept across horses grazing in the field.

"This is some house," Jack sputtered.

"Wait until you get inside," Tony said.

I sat up to get a better view. "Hell yeah, nice."

We walked up to the front porch and Shelby greeted us at the door. The four of us stepped inside a massive foyer. Off to our left was a large formal living room with sky-blue walls, a baby grand piano, pieces of sculpture and large oil paintings. I felt like we were in a museum.

We followed Shelby down the hall through a swinging door. The kitchen opened up into a den beyond it. Shelby's three friends stood at the kitchen counter with soda cans in their hands. Two of the girls giggled as we entered the room. Shelby introduced us. They were her classmates from Villa, the private-school. They wore preppy sweaters and jeans, and were definitely a notch above the public school girls we tried to make time with.

There was one girl, Marissa, with long brown hair and rosy cheeks, nice round eyes and a cute laugh. I made my way over to chat her up before Jack had a chance. I wanted to stake my claim.

The two giggling girls were introduced as Katherine and Erma. Katherine was tall and thin, with blonde hair and a pale quiet face. Erma was small and plump, with a mischievous look and a hearty laugh.

"You guys want a Coke?" Shelby walked over to the refrigerator.

Lester acted like a gentleman and opened the refrigerator door for Shelby. As she knelt down for the soda, Lester reached in over her and pulled a bottle of champagne off the top rack. He held the bottle for all to see and then tipped the bottle up in a drinking gesture.

Shelby placed a few sodas on the counter and turned to Lester. "Hey, give that to me. Are you trying to get me into trouble?" She took the champagne and held it carefully in her hands.

"My parents are celebrating their wedding anniversary," Shelby said. "They're going to drink this when they come home tonight." She looked at the label. "It's a Clos du Mesnil that they've been saving for just this occasion." She placed the bottle gently back in the fridge and handed out the sodas. Erma pulled a small bottle of rum from her bag and poured a shot into her soda can. Katherine passed the bottle around and we each carefully poured out a shot into our drinks.

Tony asked, "How long have they been married?"

"Twenty years today," Shelby said.

Erma jumped in, "It's so romantic, they still love each other after all this time. You're lucky Shelby, to have them together like that."

"They make such a cute couple," Katherine said. "I hope I'm that lucky."

"Face it, Shelby," Erma joked. "Your parents are my heroes. Here's to Ed and Jeanne!" She raised her soda in a toast and the girls clinked their cans together.

"To Ed and Jeanne!" they said.

Erma looked at the boys. "My parents got divorced two years ago. It's been a huge stinky mess."

"Yeah, but it's better than when they were always fighting," Katherine said.

"Yeah, " Erma replied, "but only because they both feel guilty. Hell, I got a new car out of it!" She let out a boisterous laugh and raised her can in salute.

We found our way into the den, sat with the girls and talked. They told us about Villa, how they didn't like the nuns, how they wish they had boys at their school. We were having a good talk, you know, just getting to know them. We didn't often get a chance to meet girls like this. It was like a different world.

After a bit of small talk, Shelby took Tony by the hand and they disappeared out to the hall. Jack joked around with Katherine and Erma, and Erma laughed really loud at Jack's jokes.

I was talking to this girl, Marissa, asking her questions and getting to know her. The whiskey and the burger and the rum had smoothed out a little. She was a refined girl with a sparkle in her eyes. She told me she wanted to be a veterinarian, and that she loved to ride horses.

Across from us Lester seemed lost. He had sat next to Katherine on the couch, but her attention was firmly on the conversation with Jack and Erma. Lester listened in, and occasionally made comments that were brushed off by the girls. Then, Lester put his hand on Katherine's knee. She shot up straight and moved. Lester watched her. His hand started fidgeting and he clasped both hands together, as if wringing them out.

Jack glanced at his watch and announced we needed to get going. "Shelby wanted us to leave before her parents get home. We don't want to cause any problems."

"I've got to take a squirt," Lester said and disappeared.

Jack went off to find Tony and Shelby. I stayed and talked to the girls, cherishing every moment. I felt as though Marissa and I had hit it off. I wanted to ask for her number, but was too shy to ask with the other girls seated nearby.

After a few minutes, Jack returned and Tony and Shelby came in laughing. "You ready to go? Where's Lester?"

"I have no clue," I replied with a shrug.

We walked to the front door and stepped out onto the porch. Down in the darkened driveway, Lester leaned against the car smoking a cigarette.

The three of us said goodbye to the girls. We gave them hugs like we'd known them for years. It all seemed very mature, on the porch of this big stately house, we felt like real gentlemen.

We walked down to the car. "What are you doing Lester?"

"Just waiting for you ladies." He flicked his cigarette butt onto the ground and stomped on it.

As Jack turned the car around, Lester said with disgust, "Private-school girls."

I just shook my head and wondered how I might find Marissa's phone number. For a moment, I convinced myself I would find a way to call her in a day or two. As we neared the end of the driveway, Jack stopped to let a car pass on the dark country road. The headlights appeared to slow down, as if wanting us to pull out ahead of them.

"Damn, this must be Shelby's folks," Jack said nervously.

"Oh shit," Tony winced. The car suddenly accelerated and I noticed the wood paneling of a station wagon as it passed by.

"Oh man, I was sure that was them," Tony said with a sigh as we pulled out onto the road.

Lester rolled down his window and a damp chill seeped in. He reached under the front seat and pulled out a bottle in the dark. I thought a shot of Wild Turkey might warm me up. Lester leaned toward the open window with the bottle and wrestled with the top until we heard the pop of a cork that scared the hell out of Jack.

"What the fuck was that?" Jack asked. Tony twisted in his seat and gasped.

"Here's to twenty years of love and marriage," Lester toasted. I watched him raise the bottle and take a prolonged swig. He wiped his lips with the back of his hand, and then he turned and held the bottle out toward me and asked, "Who's celebrating tonight?"

JOAN HILL

The Acceptance Letter

When Trudy Horn's acceptance letter arrived from Cornell, it belonged to her mother just as much. It meant that Mrs. Matilda Horn had done her job, that she had been a good mother. It meant she was free to go. She would leave Trudy's father this summer with her head held high, and she would move out before Trudy was settled into her dorm room. Eventually, the neighbors would notice odd women coming and going with Mr. Horn, and then they would know who the rat was. It would be nice for them to understand everything.

Her husband, Stuart, had no idea that she was leaving. Leaving like a heavy fruit that one day drops to the ground. *Because it was time.* No need to inform the tree. She hadn't told Trudy about her plans to leave either. For her own protection. It had always been about doing what was best for Trudy.

On Trudy's eighteenth birthday, Stuart announced that he would take their daughter to Spain for the first two weeks in August. They left on a Saturday morning, and soon after, Matilda drove to The Dream Furniture Company to arrange for the delivery of her new things. She had picked them out shortly after the news about Cornell: a queen bedroom set for herself and a single bed and dresser for Trudy, a kitchen dinette, a sofa and two end tables, five lamps. That had been a buoyant day. Matilda and a cheerful saleslady had tea while paging through books of fabric samples. The saleslady wasn't in the store this morning, and the place seemed more packed with furniture than before, so close that you had to pick a path through it. She met with an old man who smelled like saltines, who had white spittle between his lips that moved when he spoke. They sat in a room made on three sides by tall bookcases with a space for a doorway, the fourth side against doors like those of a restaurant kitchen, with porthole windows and rubber seals crumpled against the gritty floor.

"This fabric. Backorder." It seemed he might be talking to himself. "This one," he said, tapping the invoice with his thick-skinned finger. "The sofa. It's the fabric that's holding it up."

"But I made this order months ago."

"Says here we tried to call. No answer."

He turned the invoice around so she could see it right-side up. "That is not my phone number," she said. "The last digit should be a seven." He scribbled a seven over the last digit. Matilda asked when it would be ready. When he said September 16th, she wilted. Trudy would be gone by September. She pictured the empty space in her living room where the sofa should go, where she would sit next to Trudy, watching movies before she left for Cornell. Where Trudy would say that she understood why her mother had left, where she thanked her for staying all those years.

"Let me show you." The old man beckoned her to follow him, fluttering his fingers in toward his chest. She followed him to the back of the store where sofas of all styles and colors were lined up end-to-end in four or five rows, waiting for people who knew how to choose between them. "Try this one," he said as he patted a green floral. "This is the bestseller." She sat like a child on the cushion, listening as he told her how he kept this one at the front of the room on purpose, how some customers would pick it right away without even looking through the rest, and how others would look through the whole room and still come back to it. "Well, what do you think?"

She hated being pressured, hated worrying about his feelings. "It's very comfortable. It is," she said, caressing the cushion beside her. "But it's not what I want. And I'm pretty good at waiting." He shrugged.

She followed him back to the deal table. He asked her when she would like delivery, and when she told him next week he yelled out, startling Matilda. "George! Are we still doing the Murray delivery on Monday?" George appeared from behind a tall bookcase and reclined against it on his shoulder. He grinned at Matilda, revealing a gold tooth. His biceps bulged like a snake after a meal. He was tan, needed a shave and a bigger t-shirt.

"Murray switched to Thursday," George replied. His voice was deep.

"Okay, good, we'll deliver Monday. This is Mrs. ..." he looked at the invoice again, "Mrs. Horn." His eyes widened a bit as he recognized her name. "You had tea with my wife," he said. "You're new to the neighborhood." He touched her arm. "This is my son, George," and then to George, "Mrs. Horn is moving in on Penny Street with her daughter."

Matilda was shocked that he'd mentioned Trudy. She must have told his wife about her when she came to pick out the furniture. George nodded, smirked again at Matilda and flashed his green eyes. "Alright. See you then, Mrs. Horn." He left through the doors with the porthole windows, and Matilda's eyes followed the dark tattoo on the back of his neck.

The old man took her credit card and left the room. After a few moments, Matilda peeked through one of the round windows where George had gone. She saw him and two shorter men, standing around a coffee pot, laughing and smoking. George's back was to the door and he had a wallet chain hanging from his belt. The others were a collection of sprawling blue-green tattoos, crowding their arms, a spider web with an elbow at its center, a mermaid, skulls. One of them caught her eye and she returned to her seat. These were the men who were coming to her home. These men knew it was just her and her daughter. Had she mentioned Trudy's name? Had she mentioned how beautiful Trudy was? God, she couldn't remember how much she had told over the tea.

After thanking the old man, she made her way to the car, took a few breaths, and told herself that she was being ridiculous. This was an enormous step! Of course she was off balance and she should forgive herself. She chuckled, imagining delivery men wearing tuxedos. She simply had to be more reserved, more careful about what information she shared. Remembering that she had left a key with the neighbor to let the exterminator in made her cringe.

Before pulling off the lot she glanced at her pencil drawing of the two turns she needed to make to get to Penny Street, still within the free delivery radius of the Dream Furniture Company. She wanted to look again at where the furniture should go, and do some cleaning. She passed Hanes Foods (her new grocery store), a pharmacy, an aquarium supply store, a strip mall with a paperback swap, and Pete's, a bar with a free-standing neon palm tree by its entrance. She made a right at the Copely Heights Apartments onto Rand Road where there were single homes, some of them turned into businesses, others with empty front porches, their faces closed to the busy road with evergreens and roller shades.

She turned left onto Penny Street, where the row homes began. Hers was at the beginning of the third block. She turned right at the cross street and onto the driveway behind them. She remembered the green shingles on her tiny garage, a shed really, too narrow for even a small car, and hers was in better shape than most. There was an orange van backed into her space with *Norton Exterminating* on its side. Her screen door was propped open with a pesticide canister, and she decided that she wouldn't ask why he was here today, wouldn't ask what had happened to her Thursday appointment. She would handle the glitches as they came.

She parked on the other side of the driveway, against the guardrail that protected a brittle field called *Bonsall Park*.

She hoisted the vacuum cleaner out of her car, lugged it past the cartoon bugs on the side of the van, and up the three concrete stairs at the back of the house. The key was on the counter just inside the door. It was closed-up hot and the air was heavy with eggshell paint. She wished she had brought a fan.

She could hear a man's boots above her. He was whistling. She walked to the bottom of the staircase but decided to wait for him to come down on his own. She went out to the car again and carried in the mop and a bucket filled with rags and a bottle of Mr. Clean. They met in the kitchen as she came in this time. There was sweat beaded on his bald head and his uniform was zippered snugly over his egg-shaped middle. "I'll be out of your way in a minute," he said. "I'm done upstairs. I'll do the basement next and work my way out the first floor. Lickety-split." As he descended the basement stairs, Matilda decided to wait in the clear air, relieved that the heavy boots belonged to the kind of man who would say "lickety-split."

She sat on the top step of her front porch, surveying the street, pleased by the symmetry of the porches and railings, doors across from doors under a tunnel of sycamore leaves. Nothing else in her price range had included mature trees. Apart from that, the new neighborhood wasn't fancy. Here and there the sidewalks were buckled up by roots, with edges painted yellow. She hoped Trudy would like it, hoped that she would recognize the coziness.

Matilda would be cautious about meeting people. At least here the people to avoid would be easy to pick out. *Thank you, tattered window blinds. Thank you, garbage cans left at the curb.* A tall man passed her porch, without looking her way. He wore long pants despite the heat, and with an enormous, bobbing stride, he was quickly down the block. She could hear what Stuart would say about this neighborhood, about the people here. *So pedestrian. So blue collar. So canned together. Like sardines. Like cattle. Like roaches.* The exterminator rapped his knuckles on the window behind Matilda. He waved goodbye and she went upstairs.

The chain chinked against the light bulb when she pulled the string in her bedroom closet, and the fixture wobbled. The baseboard and the edges of the floor were shining wet with pesticide and a few strands of carpet that had been torn out were stuck in the wetness. She saw no point in covering the bottom of her bucket with cleaning fluid, filling it with hot water and dripping into the poison. Or trying to avoid it, looking down all the time. She would have to wait for it to dry completely before she could start. For the first time she felt like nothing mattered. She couldn't do this today. She would wait until there was enough time for the poison to do its job, until she could forget that she was mopping it up and that it was being diluted into her cleaning bucket, the concentration getting stronger with each rinse. She gave up on the upstairs, but peeked into the bathroom before going down. Smoky yellow tile with a black border. There was nothing she could do to make it work, not like she had thought when she first looked through the house.

She went back to the kitchen and picked the rags out of the bucket, then put the bucket in the sink, turned on the hot water and dumped in some cleaner. She pulled on her gloves and wiped down the countertop. She wiped up the stovetop, and realized she would need toothpicks to push the grease out of the grooves around the dials. She looked up at the ceiling and the walls and her frustration grew at the little bit she was doing. She wanted to start at the top and do it completely the first time, but she didn't even have a chair to stand on. She had no paper or anything to write with, so a list began repeating itself in her head with each wipe: *toothpicks, stepladder, fan.* She knelt to wipe out a cabinet and once she reached in she added contact paper to her list, wanting to cover the grainy shelf with something, anything. Sweat was beginning to collect in her hairline and her hands were slippery in the gloves. The skin of her knees ground thin between her weight and the floor, forced into the texture lines of the linoleum. She added knee pads to her list. She couldn't do any more today. She hadn't eaten breakfast and she thought about the deli at the corner and a sandwich, and about trying to enjoy the newness of the neighborhood while she still could.

She smelled the remains of the fire before she saw the burned out deli. She followed the rubbery caution tape off the curb into a fire hose puddle. The blackness struck Matilda as a color found nowhere else, and she stared at the silvery ash scaled over the wood as if it belonged to some exotic fish. The paint on the metal shelving was puckered. A *Cold Beer* sign was blackened at the bottom, but the word *cold* was still blue, still the color of cold. The smell and the wetness beneath it stuck inside her nose in the spot where the cartilage ends and the bone begins, blocking everything else. She would smell it any time a breeze carried the blackness under the sycamore trees to her door, until a bulldozer came and scraped this place into a dumpster, and maybe until several heavy rains after that.

Walking back, she tried to recall whether she'd heard the sirens from across town. She hadn't watched the news the night before, and felt robbed by missing what would surely be the talk of this block for years to come. She imagined the flames and smoke, the pressure in the hoses lying heavy on the street and leaking at the connections, helmets and boots swarming, the spectators in their night clothes, and herself among them. And now in the daylight it was over and there was no deli for her to get a sandwich, or for her and Trudy to get a pizza, and she wondered if they would ever rebuild it. She was starving.

She passed through the empty row home, a hallway back to her car, slowed only by the ritual of unlocking and locking the doors. She was halfway across the tiny yard when a voice called out "You can't park there!" Matilda turned to see her neighbor with the penciled eyebrows, the one she had left the key with. "You can't park there. They are very strict about that." Matilda explained about the exterminator parking in her spot, about moving in. "And thanks for holding the key," she added. The woman only frowned and closed her door. Matilda stared at the spot where her face had been, where it had cut her off. She tried to stop whispering *bitch* as she wiped bird shit from her car door handle, tried to remind herself that it would be best to get along with the woman on the other side of the wall. She balled up the rag and placed it against the garage door in the corner. *Trash cans. She needed trash cans.* She started the car, boiling even in the shade, opened all the windows and turned on the air conditioner. She turned her crude map around to reorient herself for her ride home. It must have been the feel of the paper that made her look into the bottom of the door pocket where she saw a pencil. She called herself an idiot for not realizing that she could have started her list after all and scribbled *trashcans, stepladder, fan, knee pads, contact paper.* She thought how much more interesting her list would be if she added *rat poison, shovel, lime.* But instead she wrote: *I hate you, Stuart. You fucking liar.*

As she drove back home the curbs fell away, the edges softened. Between the town and the suburbs were fields of corn and wooded areas, the plants here merely tamed, mowed back from the road. Once she turned into the development the trees and shrubs were suddenly planned and placed, for shade, for privacy; as specimens. She had to admit that it was still home as she started up the driveway that wrapped around one side of the pond at the front of the property and rose slightly until it met the custom wooden doors of the three-car garage. She had actually gasped when she saw this house for the first time.

She left both sets of keys in the mudroom, which was larger than her new kitchen. She washed her hands in the kitchen sink, and thought about needing hand soap dispensers for her own place as she dried them. She opened the enormous wood-paneled refrigerator and noticed the interior for the first time since it was new in the kitchen. The glass shelves were deep, the lighting was complete and professional. She retrieved the egg salad she had made for Trudy's lunch the day before, and thought about the refrigerator on Penny Street: its metal racks, how it stood out in its own compartment at the end of the cabinets, how no one in that neighborhood could ever afford to change that. She thought about her knees on the linoleum again, when she was wiping up the dirt that was beneath it. She scooped the egg salad onto a roll and bit in.

She began to notice the difference in things after she met Stuart. He'd always had money. She worked at the travel agency where he used to book his trips, usually only three or four days out. Their first date was her first whiff of a new car. She worried about scuffing the ivory leather, and when Stuart closed her door, it made a sound like the thud of a large cushion hitting the floor, sealing her away. That same summer there was something wrong with the door latch on her Chevette, and she had to slam it several times before it would stick, the hinge groaning each time, and her brother said *why don't you oil it, you asshole* — one of the last things he said to her before he left for boot camp.

It had been easy to say yes when Stuart asked her to book tickets for both of them. She remembered feeling that she deserved it, that she had been good, had the looks, the right morality to enjoy the better things. A hand had been extended to her and she was glad to pull herself up. On her birthdays, Stuart gave her gift certificates, and she found out what it was like to be comforted in front of mirrors in salons and upscale clothing stores, where a perfumed stylist or assistant would ask if you'd like something to drink, or hand a different size or color over the dressing room door. This was not the way her mother had shopped. There was no conversation when her mother needed a new dress for a wedding or a funeral. It was not about the joy or the somberness; it was about the money. While her mother searched for something suitable, sliding every hanger in the dress-up section at *Carlita's Thrift Shop*, Matilda would pull the smooth pins out of the loops in the store's thin carpet, beg to know when they could go home, and hide in the center of a clothing rack, rocking her miserable, waiting body against the heavy clothes.

Matilda finished her sandwich, drank some water and began to relax, as if her body thanked her for the familiar return, and the headache that had been creeping up behind her eyes faded and her stomach felt warm and cheerful. She took a long shower and settled onto her favorite sofa, whispering *damn it* for the backordered fabric only once before she drifted off.

It was growing dark when she awoke. She tried to remember her dream. Stuart was in it, wagging his finger at her, telling her she couldn't do...something. But that was all before her mind returned to her list. She started for the basement. Her fingertips played over the tops of the wine bottles protruding from the rack that lined the stairwell. She made a random choice and set the bottle upright on the stair to wait for her.

In the basement she found two fans. She chose the oscillating fan and carried it up the stairs, picking up the wine on her way and placing it on the kitchen table. She put the fan in her car, along with a stepladder she found in the garage. She returned to the kitchen, unscrewed the cork and poured herself a glass. It was red, dry, delicious.

In the basement again, she found the vacuum cleaner bags, several vacuum hose attachments she didn't even know existed, and an extra broom and dustpan. After searching the shelves for several minutes, she even found knee pads. These items seemed like precious inventory when she released them from her arms into the car. She drained her first glass of wine and poured another, thinking about the thick, black power lines running up to the back of her new house, the caution tape, the bird shit. About her pride and taking as little as possible from this house. About so many details. Taking things began to seem like the right thing to do, the smart thing to do. She wasn't going to take large items. She was taking crumbs.

She went back for half a case of toilet paper, a can of interior trim paint, a package of mixed grit sandpaper and several expensive paintbrushes. She selected a hammer, two screwdrivers, and some picture hangers from the tool box.

Several more bottles of wine from the staircase. She piled everything on the kitchen table. She sipped her wine and reviewed the useful junk, thinking of being reduced to it, being reduced by it. When she helped Trudy pack for Cornell, she told her that the less she had to lug around and look after, the better. This was an entirely new idea for Trudy, who had never wanted, or been without comfort, entertainment, nutrition.

Matilda's thoughts were sliding through the effects of the wine, and things seemed sad and funny all at once. She thought about the awkward time between being a child and being an adult, when everyone is waiting for you to become something, to go somewhere. You notice the four walls in your bedroom and you become painfully aware of your confinement. You are living at your parents' house, and it's the last place you want to be.

She finished her second glass of wine and a kind of panic set in. She had an even less attractive place for Trudy to return to. An unfamiliar place, a place that wasn't home. It would smell different, the light would be different. She would have to gather things with a new kind of list in her head.

She began to collect items that Trudy would want: the blender for her smoothies and milkshakes, her favorite coffee mugs, the throw blanket she always used in front of the television. Her favorite snow globe from the collection. The painting of a blond girl holding a little white dog. Matilda picked out Trudy's CDs, the CD player and the speakers, and carried them all to the kitchen. Let them be missing here, not at her home. Let some gap be felt when they walk back through this door in two weeks.

She made her way to her daughter's bedroom, where Trudy's conversations with friends were private and her girlish body had been doing what it does: looking at itself, trying things on, leaving lipstick on the mirror, being Trudy, becoming Trudy. All the dreams and trying were entering a new phase, one where Stuart wouldn't count as much, where Trudy was becoming her own person, truly separate from them both. It was right, the both of them leaving, as long as Matilda had the same bond with Trudy. As long as she could lure her to Penny Street.

Trudy's room was a shell, with boxes lined around her dresser. Her closet was open and empty except for three unwanted tops that hung misshapen. Matilda crossed the room to Trudy's trophy shelf. She picked up one of them, feeling the seamless human figure in the crotch of her fingers. It was so cheap compared to its symbolism. She had prepared her daughter, had encouraged her, nurtured her through all her experiences. The trophies were evidence of a capable girl. Matilda placed the trophy back with the others.

The crisp remains of two pill bugs littered the window sill, and Matilda held up the waste can and blew them out of the corner into the can. Beneath the built-in window seat were Trudy's sketchbook and pencils, her journals and her favorite schoolwork from high school. There was a scrapbook with magazine pictures of skinny models pasted into it, most of them with angry, sexy eyes over pouting lips. There was a shoebox with every card she had ever gotten from Matilda. These belonged to both of them and they belonged on Penny Street. She placed the box on the bed and looked through them. At the bottom there was a blue envelope. "For T" was written on it. It had been handed to Trudy. Matilda pulled the card out.

The front of it showed a matador beside a charging bull, his cloak furled out above its head. Spears penetrated the bull's shoulders. Its front legs were thrown out straight, its tongue held stiffly in its mouth, and its eyes showed the moment when sure revenge turned to surprise. Matilda opened the card and read: *Happy Birthday Trudy! Your father and I can't wait to celebrate with you in Spain! We'll go shopping at Fuencarra and Hortaleza! Hugs and kisses, Rebecca*

On Sunday, Matilda packed a lunch and cleaned the house on Penny Street. The poison was dry and she dumped seven buckets of dirty water down the toilet.

On Monday, George and the tattooed men from the Dream Furniture Company double-parked their box truck on Penny Street and hauled the furniture in, their hands on her queen mattress, their sweaty faces for the mattress to lean against as the one behind crouched and grunted when they worked it through the front door, then squished it up the stairwell and bent it through the turn at the top of the stairs. Thank God for flexibility and plastic covers. The dinette came in with the edges of the table and curved chairs protected with Styrofoam paper taped around them. They put it in the kitchen against the long wall in the only spot it could go, not across from either the dishwasher or the refrigerator. After they left she hated the red color, and the fact that it took up more room than she had pictured, even though she had measured, and that it would always be awkward to walk around it in the kitchen.

The day before the return flight from Spain, Matilda went back to the big house in the suburbs for the last time to leave a note for Trudy:

Dear Trudy, I have left your father. But not you, never you. Please, please visit me as soon as you can – 612 Penny Street. I'll always love you. Mom

P.S. I guess you've tried to protect me. I can accept that.

VIRGINIA BEARDS

A Hunt Tea

The Loon Hills Hounds. There are no *Gavia immer* loons and few hills. Nevertheless for 85 years, generation after generation, the hunt members have effortlessly lived up to the Loon appellation. Keenly aware that foxhunting is the most fun you can have with your clothes on, they ride hard, party accordingly and give only a sideways glance to the limb, life and home wrecking episodes brought on by hunt field antics fueled by daring, drink, and the sexual imperative.

Mud splattered, teeth chattering, Amelia untacked Bosco, threw a faded green cooler over his back and headed to the hunt house for the after-hunt tea. Her dirty rowel spurs and damp boots pinched her feet but she had no alternative — no boot jack, no spare shoes. "Oh hell, this won't be the first time I've gone home sobbing, soggy or half-way hobbling." The boots and spurs would have to stay on and Bosco would have to shiver in the horse trailer. She was not one to miss a party. Inside the hunt house kitchen she cosied herself over to the Franklin stove that Jake, enduring kennel man, had stoked and brought to red hot two hours before the long mournful notes of the huntsman's horn signaled "going home." As she warmed herself she eyed the coffee, wine, rum, Irish whiskey and waited for the others to arrive while fantasizing about the scarlet coated, square shouldered, strong backed hunt guest she had been riding behind for most of the day. That back! It made her believe in God, and men.

The kitchen door banged open, a pack of hunters rushed through. Mud on stock ties that had been pristine at 11am, hunt coats spotted and torn from splashes and crashes, the usual victim calling for a bandage or at least some Bactine. Most of the gentlemen headed straight for the drinks table, the ladies for the loo with their makeup bags.

"Hey Amelia, meet Clifford Jespersen, my buddy from Boston," said Danny Keats, Amelia's longtime hunt sidekick and husband of one of her few women friends.

"Hullo. Nice to meet your front after staring at your back for so many hours out there. What kind of bit did you have in your guy's mouth? Seemed vigorous but remarkably controlled. I like that sort of thing."

"A double wire twisted snaffle, might seem cruel but in good hands it's right for a strong mount. Wouldn't want to go out in a Pelham. Ladies bit!" he added knowing full well that the present — hmm lady? — no, woman, probably rode in just that.

Sexist snot thought Amelia as she headed off to the white wine unaware that she was being followed by he whom she had earlier christened "the exemplary back."

"What are you having? I'm going for the Irish Whiskey, the Jamesons."

"I'll take it too" said Amelia, suddenly realizing that white wine like the Pelham bit was too much of a lady's thing. In fact she wasn't feeling ladylike at all. Ice and two finger's worth quickly filled their glasses. She checked Clifford's face as they said "cheers," swallowed and felt the instantaneous rush of 80-proof alcohol through her limbs. His back she realized was definitely more alluring than his front, however he had unusual eyes — brown with some gold flecks, only slightly bloodshot. Straight nose and a decent enough smile. As they walked through the various hunt parlors framed with photographs of hunt members galloping, jumping, crashing, and decorously parading hounds around a show ring, Amelia rattled on about who was who, where that covert with the gigantic coop is above which someone was snapped airborne as his soulful eyed horse stood confused on the take-off side. But actually, neither was particularly interested. They were passing time before heading back to the Irish whiskey, to whatever might follow.

In the kitchen now warmed to 78 degrees, jammed with anecdotal and marginally inebriated fox chasers, Amelia pilots Clifford to the drinks table. Getting into the feel of the thing, they fill their glasses and say *sláinte* while looking steadily at each other. Drifting over to the buffet with its stuffed eggs, blue cheese dip with vegetables, pasta salad, chili, and a whole raft of other Tagament promoting dishes courtesy of the hunt ladies, Amelia turns slightly green. Clifford, equally disinclined for the fare, leads her back to the drinks. In the spirit of scientific investigation they pour Bushmills, completely unaware of the ongoing competition between the distilleries of Northern Ireland and the Irish Republic.

"So what d'you think of us Loons?" asks Amelia quickly refilling her glass, this time with Tullamore Dew. Clifford silently considers her query and thinks, "Well, I'm seeing one loon here and she's okay, quite okay."

"I'll show you the upstairs. It's where there's the only decent photo of me and Bosco in the hunt field."

Clifford is on for this, fully aware of what the second floor of an early 19th century stone house in the Loon country will hold. They tour four bedrooms, each hung with boringly repetitive hunt photos. Finally coming to hers, he politely admires the framed shot of Amelia and Bosco, ignores her heels up, roached back, the horse on his forehand and a look of abject terror on Amelia's face. They then enter the presumed "master bedroom" even though it's been almost a decade since the bedroom or its water bed have received a guest, or guests.

Feet now aching and burning after the kitchen heat, the steep wooden stairs and her sweaty socks, Amelia joyously collapses on the bed. Her incipient lust for Clifford, his back or front, adds to her enthusiasm. Where upon he of the glorious back tumbles on top of her. Impossible thrashing begins. Belts, stretch riding breeches and oh my god — there's no fucking way to get them off! Amelia's custom made Dehner boots with their elaborate spur "lock system," an absurd blockade to carnal pleasure. At the same time she senses that while one thing is inflating another is deflating. The Master's pleasure bed, holdover from his bachelor days, is slowly leaking, punctured by her rowel spurs. Amelia and Clifford of the stellar back are sinking, sinking, and sinking. Getting inappropriately wet.

Downstairs sweaty, exuberant and voracious foxhunters jam the food table. Danny, however, is perplexed. Where's Amelia? As he half-heartedly grazes about the buffet envisioning lurid Amelia scenarios, he feels something cold plink onto his left hand. Another plink follows, this time making a small indentation in the clam dip. He looks up. A patch of the ceiling directly overhead oozes and weeps. As a plumbing contractor he knows all about water in old houses — where it comes from where it goes, how it clogs drains, eats pin holes in copper, rots out under sink cabinets and consumes the linings of hot water heaters. But this has him stumped. He is perfectly aware that there are no plumbing fixtures in the room above, but knowing Amelia equally well — her diversions, evasions and weaknesses as complex as those in any 18th century farm house — he realizes that she and Clifford have gone AWOL. Deciding to investigate he is nearly knocked off his feet on the stairs as a phalanx of young hunters who consider themselves gentlemen but are decidedly not so at this moment, whooshes down the stairs gleefully yelling "ware hole, ware hole" and "tally ho!" Charging into the master bedroom Danny's suspicions are made flesh. It is the closing scene in a third rate French farce. The soaking pair struggles to extricate themselves from a tangle of deflated waterbed fabric, ripped britches and torn sheets while a sodden Amelia laughingly taunts an indecently disheveled and dour faced Clifford, his glorious back totally forgotten, with a raucous, "Welcome to the Loon Hill Hounds!"

VIRGINIA BEARDS

Fall Out and Frock Coats

As a *"Japanese City's Desperate Cry Resonates Around the World"* (*New York Times*, March 15, 2011), I'm sitting on Bosco in the opening mêlée of a mid-March hunt watching horses swirl, riders adjust their tack and under the cover of chat try to conceal their jitters about the big—some might say even "life threatening"—fences ahead.

"What did you think of the Clydesdale cross at Ryan's? A weight carrier but could he stand up to the Somerset country?"

"Even if he could, he's not very classy. Don't like to show up on a goat. Doesn't look good."

"Do you think," asks a fifty-something woman to no one in particular, "those elevator bits Bruce told me about would work on a really hard-mouthed horse?"

Looks matter and that's why I'm sweating just now. Not an official color-wearing Somerset Hunt member ("navy blue frock coat with white facings") according to the National Hunt Register, I'm a visitor wearing my heavy Loon Hills Hounds hunt coat ("forest green with cream facings") even though the day is threateningly warm. Hunt decorum. Big deal. But I'm not quite with it.

I'm in a cloud of nuclear gloom when my doomsday reverie is broken by a sixty something gentleman wearing a Loon Hills frock coat. Odd I think. Never seen this guy before and I've been a Loonatic for eight seasons. Glancing at his chestnut's fetlocks, I realize that the horse belongs to Michael, a retired foxhunter and former Philadelphia lawyer.

Its fetlocks, the Dun and Bradstreet of the horse world, tell the story in bullet points and bold print. Many seasons, hard ridden. Next it dawns on me that its rider looks like a younger Michael as he introduces himself as Steffen Forar. Michael's son, but definitely without the European courtliness or *savoir faire*. Tight back, rigid jaw.

"How's Michael," I ask. "Miss seeing him out here. Always good company especially on the slow days when talking kept us from boredom, wind chill, hypothermia, drowning, you name it."

"He's fine for being eighty-nine. Gave me his Loon Hills coat, said my off-the-rack black Melton's too shabby." I didn't say anything about this son's unearned official hunt coat. I really didn't care, but knowing Michael to be a stickler for hunt decorum minutiae I was a bit surprised.

"Seems to fit you perfectly," I said as I sidled off to re-enter my geo-environmental black fog. As I waited for the hounds to go to covert I recalled Michael telling me that Steffen was a tax lawyer which he thought must be deadly dull but that Steffen enjoyed "dotting the i's and crossing the t's." This amused me because Michael himself is a detailist — the correct tack, the precise form for an RSVP to a hand written invitation, the perceived "best" novel by Marguerite Yourcenar, the sequence of Crystal Night, the Anschuss, the annexing of Silesia, the proper pronunciation of the Duke of Buccleuch's surname....Yes, Michael's mind ranged widely and eccentrically. And this endeared him to me. He sought out conversation that one wouldn't expect in the hunt field.

As we jogged along Steffen reappeared beside Bosco and me.

"I think last night's rain might make for good scent today." Duh, I didn't respond. He tried again a bit later to break through my dark mood by telling me something about horse trailer hitches. Definitely not his father's son in the social department. I was relieved but also mystified when another new face, this one in a generic black hunt coat, joined us introducing himself as a member of the Loon Hills Hounds. I had never seen him out with the Loons. His black eyes, pitch dark velvet hunt cap and anthracite glistening boots were startling. His turn-out impressive. I figured he had yet to be invited to wear the Loon Hills green coat. That takes time.

"I just joined the Loon Hills this season and don't get out except on Saturdays. Guess we've missed each other? I take it you're seasoned Loon members?" There was a slight edge to his voice and a hint of aggressiveness as he eyed Steffen's green coat.

"Actually," Steffen replied, "this is my father's coat. I'm not a Loon Hiller, but my father was for many years." I could see BC (blackcoat) was perplexed. Michael's bespoke frock coat was handsome. I knew how many fittings he had for it and what he paid. You just don't get Frank Hall of Market Harborough by Royal Appointment to the Prince of Wales to run you up such on the cheap. Anyway, as these gentlemen thought back forty years they worked out that they'd been within two years of each other at Penn law school. This conversation took time. Many verbal circles. They reminded me of two dogs nosing around one another trying to size each other up prior to wagging their tails or lunging at each other's necks.

I thought back to when I had been invited to wear the Loon Hills official coat. I was just twenty and although a newcomer from the West Coast — comically perceived of by some in the East as a region of frontier gaucheries — I did know how to ride properly, look people in the eye, shake hands, and decently turn-out Bosco and myself. I also had read Mr. Wadsworth's *Riding to Hounds in America* (1962). Anyway, I declined the highly recommended Frank Hall custom made garment. I couldn't afford it. To me its extravagance made about as much sense as that of an expensive coffin. Highly finished and bulging. Besides, I secretly thought that some of the hunt women in their Frank Hall coats looked like they were wearing heavy, lumpy green bathrobes. I eventually bought a well-fitting forest green hunt coat off-the-rack in Ireland and hand-sewed on the required cream felt facings. It was perfect — not at all baggy or too big. No one but Michael knew it was counter-feit.

Somehow I couldn't get away from the Black Coat. I even began to fantasize that BC was the personification of my mood, my private version of Eliot's "objective correlative." He and Steffen kept riding up behind Bosco and me in a peculiar riff on kind-sticking-with-kind based, I suppose, on our Loon Hill ties. I glanced back a couple of times to see how my self-appointed legal escorts were doing. Steffen's face was a mix of focus and pleasure while BC, galloping dangerously close, had his coal dark eyes riveted on Steffen's green back and was biting his lower lip. At the checks he continued staring at Steffen's hunt coat, now mud splashed but still elegant. Obsessed? A new form of fetishism? Was his behavior a grown-man's take on the sixth grade boy who rips the high end sneakers off his wimpy classmate? I couldn't work it out but it was creepy. For the rest of the day I tried to ignore those two and forget the looming international problem far beyond the Somerset Hounds' greening spring gallops, coverts, and diving swallows.

The hunt ended at 2:30 with the huntsman's mournful notes of the "going home." Un-tacking, I saw the two lawyers trot up, stiffly dismount and, following the strict script of hunt decorum, equally stiffly thank the Master for "showing" them "good sport." I didn't hang around. I now had two more problems. Stomach and bladder. I headed for the comforts of a Burger King, a Whopper for me and a small fries with ketchup for Bosco. Picking up our order at the drive-thru window and pulling into the parking lot, I popped out with my bag of salty fries splashed with ketchup and hand fed them to Bosco through the trailer door before settling down in my truck to enjoy the burger. I had just arranged my Whopper and Coke plus about fifteen napkins on my lap and the truck seat and begun to remove the wrapping when my cell phone rang. It was Michael.

"Amelia, what went on in the hunt? Steffen just called and said some surly lawyer type followed him all day and afterward offered him $200 for his—I mean my—Loon Hills Hounds hunt coat. Incredible nerve! He implied that Steffen didn't have the right to wear it!" I stayed silent and let Michael rattle on. "Well perhaps he doesn't but I thought it would be better than his old black coat. So who was he?"

"I don't know, I forgot his name. Just think of him as BC, for black coat. I was preoccupied with more abstract concerns."

"Huh?"

"Well, Fukushima Daiichi for one thing, our Chernobyl to the west."

"I certainly hope I haven't made Steffen look like an imposter by giving him my hunt coat. Good turn-out's important. Anyway I like the idea of passing on my Loon Hills coat to my oldest son. It seems the correct thing to do. But maybe I better check with the Somerset and Loon Hills Masters to see that I haven't broken any hunt rules." My god, I thought, here's an eighty-nine year old fussing about the so-called legalities of a hunt coat he believes he has bequeathed to his sixty year old son who in turn seems to have run home to papa after a disturbing encounter in the hunt with another sixty year old lawyer.

While Bosco impatiently kicked at his trailer wall and I bit into my Whopper, Michael kept on about the rights and wrongs of his outsourced frock coat and BC's presumptuousness. My hunger and, I suppose, politeness (or was it indifference?) kept me from interrupting. Finally he said he thought he would try to clarify the "legal points" about the situation by calling up Richard Evans, confident that the Somerset Master of Hounds, "a true gentleman, always respectful of good form," would know "exactly how to dot the i's and cross the t's" in this matter. Hmm, I thought, Michael's favorite figure of speech. I'd heard him use it frequently. An index to his worldview? He added that he'd already looked at Mr. Wadsworth's manual but didn't say what he'd found. I'd been barely able to conceal a gasp when he said "legal points." Was he in a courtroom or on the playground discussing rules with another thirteen year old? At any rate Michael's concept of some sort of Supreme Hunt Authority took ahold. He abruptly hung up, saying he'd let me know what the Master "decreed."

When the phone rang at 9:30 that night I recognized the careful phrasing of Michael's quirkily graceful English as soon as I said hello.

"Good evening Amelia. Thought I'd give you a report, a post mortem so to speak. I think I interrupted Richard at his dinner. He was a little abrupt. But I think it's acceptable for Steffen to hunt with the Somerset Hounds in my Loon Hills coat. That black coat carpet bagger that tailed him all day will just have to wait to be asked to wear the Loon Hills colors." Hmm, I thought...and when was Steffen formally asked to wear the Loon Hills colors? He's not even a hunt member.

"What exactly did Richard say?"

"Well, I told him about what happened as well as I could piece it together from Steffen. I did mention that Wadsworth seems rather severe on 'the right to wear hunt colors,' but I'm going to check on Monday with the Masters of Foxhounds Association of America in Middleburg about hunt coat rules and, you know, precedence. Wadsworth's a bit dated. Anyway, Richard didn't say much—I even wondered if we'd been disconnected. Then I heard him swallow or gulp something, and after a very long pause he blurted out, 'I don't give a fuck what people wear in the hunt field!'"

Michael's slight laugh combined prudish shock and *au courrant* amusement. Myself, I felt stuck in an endlessly looping film noir starring three Philadelphia lawyers, a smoldering nuclear reactor, and a world of strontium 90 infused food.

VIRGINIA BEARDS

No Good Deed....

Everyone acknowledges that Alice Warren is an accomplished hunt rider, not the least herself. The daughter of a New Hampshire school teacher, she has the slight New England catch-in-her-voice that makes one wonder, well, why so uptight? Because with a few notable exceptions (and Alice is one), for the most part the Loon Hillers are casual, jokey and good humored. They go out for the fun—they "hunt to ride" rather than "ride to hunt." Their perspective is egalitarian or, crudely put, who cares what you do, just don't get in my way with your: a) balky, b) kicking, c) hot item just off the track who's never seen a jump before. You have the right to break your neck, arm or whatever. We're not school marms. Alice, however, is different. She corrects anyone who owns less land than the Warrens or who is not from an "old family" in the Loon Hills country.

Her time as a Pony Club District Coordinator might explain her approach to hunting. When I joined the Loon Hill Hunt at 18, I was the constant target of her censorious glances and tidbits of advice offered with that perpetual catch-in-her-voice. But I didn't care. To me the hunt was a circus: colorful, roaring and hugely entertaining. Better than P.T. Barnum, A.J. Ringling or any of those European circuses that my godfather blabs about, his hobby being circus life, historical and modern. Guess some of his passion rubbed off on me, for foxhunting is a three-Ringer with the added feature of 100% audience participation. My eye is always on the center ring, so if Alice wants to run a snarky little sideshow devoted to hunt riding decorum according to the *United States Pony Club Handbook* who cares? I focus on the Loon Hill lions and tigers, the swirling horses, hounds and the well-dressed ringmaster. I mean, huntsman.

My family moved to the Pennsylvania Loon Hill country from eastern Washington State where my father and his brother farmed hundreds of acres of "peas," that means soybeans in the Palouse region where we lived. On my twelfth birthday, my first one in Pennsylvania, my godfather, Jonathan Worthington, who had promoted our relocation to the East, gave me a Stubben bridle and a thirteen hand pony that I promptly named Spit. He told me I would now be ready to join the local Pony Club. I blew off his advice. I've never much gone in for anything organized or regimented. Pony Club to me meant Girl Scouts minus those ugly green uniforms and being bossed around by grown-up women devoted to community service. I later realized that most of their husbands worked for the E.P. Blondel Industries and that their wives' activities as unpaid E.P. Blondel team players could make their year-end reviews more "robust." In this Tri-State area (Pennsylvania, Delaware, Maryland) devotion to the health and image of the E. P. Blondel community seemed to be of major importance. Never mind that the cancer rates in Blondel dominated Delaware are the highest in the USA. E. P. does not stand for Environmental Protection. I was not in the Palouse anymore.

I learned to ride by hanging-out at a western hacking stable in Ridley Park, an unfashionable part of Delaware County. My parents, busy with their own fairly colorful lives, didn't interfere. As long as I came home happy each evening with no chipped teeth and nothing dislocated or broken they let me be free. At the Bar XR Stable I had one trait that made me queen of the barn rats—I could stay on anything that Tex, the stable manager, put me on. Spit had taught me well. I just sat there quietly and enjoyed the ride—lurching, diving, bucking, rearing, whatever. (Equation: lack of fear = lack of imagination.) I now know from eight years with the Loons, the horrors of what might happen to almost anyone on a frightened, confused or pissed-off horse. But the long and short of it is I never did study equestrian "technique."

When I first went out with the Loon Hill Hounds this fact seemed to drive Alice nuts. There may have been other factors fueling her animosity such as my naive approach to unearned rank in the hunt field. I rode in the first flight from the first day. A box seat at the circus for me every time! Otherwise, why bother? Then there was Alice's "turn-out" obsession. She dressed to perfection by the standards of Mr. Wadsworth's definitive guide, *Riding to Hounds in America.* Correctness is paramount with Alice. Her mouse brown hair is always so tightly netted that when she takes off her hunt derby, from her neck above she looks like she wandered in from a hospital Food Service department. You could do your hair and makeup in the mirror-like reflection of her highly polished calfskin boots. Obviously, I wasn't in her league and probably never would be. I do, however, know how to put up my long blonde hair in a proper chignon and cover it with a pretty crocheted white net so that not too many strands and wisps escape. Danny says that Alice sometimes glowers at my long legs and relaxed "hunt seat." I'm not so sure about that though.

My cell phone rang on Friday morning while I was hunting rats in our barn with my bow-legged terrier Trisket. It was Danny, an exuberant Danny.

"Hey Amelia, the Loons are having a by-day and we're all going to hunt Fair Meadows at 11am. Can you make it?"

"Silly question, 'course I can. Bosco's a bit fuzzy — haven't clipped him yet, been putting it off. But I'll be there." I turned off my cell, grabbed the Murphy's Oil Soap and went to work on my bridle. It was 9:45 already. A little too vigorous on the throatlatch, I completely ripped it from the headstal. Shit! The leather was old and thin and had been much replaced and re-stitched over the years to fit the increasingly larger horses I graduated to after Spit. What post-em notes are to the office secretary, baling twine is to the horsewoman, so taking some florescent orange twine from the hay stall, I tied a neat little square knot and reattached the throatlatch to Bosco's headstal. I got some brown Kiwi and dabbed my baling twine mend. It was a bit smeary but the knot no longer glared and flashed like a caution light. I moved on to my saddle and boots. Next I pulled a resentful Bosco out of the field, extracting burdock burrs from his mane as we walked to the barn where I stuck him in the wash stall, dampened a rag and scrubbed his four white socks. I also wiped the rag over his coat. This short cut would get you kicked out of the United States Pony Club. Not sure why rub rags are a Pony Club sin, but the overlap between the acronyms of Pony Club and Politically Correct is suggestive. Anyway, boots spiffed-up with an equally illegal Express Shine Black Sponge, I dressed, relieved to find my stock tie okay, if not immaculate. The lint roller redeemed my hunt coat. I loaded Bosco and we were off to Fair Meadows. My turn-out was definitely not up to the standards of Charles and Camilla or Alice, but fine with me.

I had forgotten it was Veterans Day (apparently the Master had too) but there was a big field of last minute riders summoned by last minute emails and phone calls. Of course Alice Warren was there as was her daughter Molly, and Boyd, Molly's fiancé. There was nothing last minute looking about Alice and her mount. Both were superbly turned-out. The Warren group was a mixed threesome — the engaged pair relaxed and the mother-in-law-to-be looking deadly serious, if not to say grim. While detaching Bosco's lead line from the metal loop inside the trailer, I heard an imperious catch-in-the-throat voice from the big horse van parked next to me.

"No! Don't take Eagle out first! Pluto can't be left alone. Can't believe you've forgotten. Pluto will panic."

"Sorry Mom, I just wanted to get us all going, we're a little late you know."

Unloading Bosco, I noticed Molly imperceptibly shaking her head and covertly grimacing at Boyd as if to say "that's how she is, ignore it." I mounted Bosco and rode off to the other field members. Matriarchy in action depresses me. On joining the field waiting for the hounds to be sent to covert, Boyd and Molly got some more strong half-halts from Alice.

"Boyd, your bridle is a bit low, take it up a hole or you'll never be able to hold Ramer. Check your girth Molly, looks loose." I rode away from the Warren group because Bosco was ping-ponging about in anticipation of careening around behind hounds working over nearly ten thousand acres bristling with foxes.

The hounds were cast and they streaked down the long open slope where we had parked the trailers and vans, entered an oak wood and crossed the Little Deer Creek which snakes through the Fair Meadows hunt country. Horses and hounds love the Little Deer; timid riders and turn-out freaks do not—the former get scared and splashed, the latter besmirch their custom made boots and frock coats. The horses fresh and pulling in their first few minutes of open country, the hunting horn sending the hounds on, and the Master and whips shouting "huic to 'im," "huic to 'im" caused all hearts to step up the beat.

Danny, riding at a fast trot just ahead of me, called back, "Hey Amelia, here comes our favorite 'men-from-the-boys wheat-from-the chaff' in-and-out!" Danny and I joke that this combination jump had been set-up by a secret gang of professional show ring jump riders eager to school their horses in the countryside. It requires three perfect strides between the "in" and the "out." Done correctly there is no finer thing. You fly, you soar! And your brain doesn't get over it for the next two hours—you riff on the Pegasus combination and effortlessly "air" the day's remaining jumps. On the other hand, if you mess-up, you crash or just plain stop and, equally stressful, feel the pressure of the hunt field behind you, waiting, circling, and judging.

The field master takes the Pegasus combination Steinkraus perfectly and so do Ed and Jan, the latter quickly spitting out a fireball candy before going into the obstacle. Smart move, this is not the time for a Heimlich maneuver on

a windpipe lodged fireball. Then Alice and her retinue —
clunk, whack, bang and the sounds of iron-shod hooves hitting oak 2x4 boards — get through.

"Boyd, give Ramer more rein over the jumps. He needs
it for balance." No response from Boyd but if I were to put
the scene in the graphic novel I'm working on, there would
be a big balloon over his head jammed with all the symbols
from the keyboard that are not in the alphabet.

Because the hounds lost the scent, the huntsman called
them in and headed for the next covert. The field slowed to a
walk, someone lit a cigarette and fireballs were passed
around by Janey who is addicted to them and likes to pro-
mote her habit.

Gossiping, flirting, joking, discussing bits, bridles and
saddles, we all went along sucking on our fireballs, turning
our tongues and lips bright red, under the skeptical eye of
Alice who, as usual, had declined Janey's hospitality. We
worked our way toward a meander in the Little Deer Creek.
As we approached the water, Alice turned to Boyd and said,

"Be careful on the bridge coming up, Ramer's crossed it
before but he avoids puddles whenever he can."

The creek was high, the low walkway bridge for hikers,
mountain bikers and horse riders was under water by about
six inches. Alice, confident as ever, rode Pluto down the low
bank to the bridge, stepped onto the first of its wooden
planks and turned her head around, ratcheting her torso at
least ninety degrees, to check on her daughter and future
son-in-law negotiating the slippery bank. Glancing briefly at
Boyd's glowering face and Molly's tense jaw, in her Pony
Club mom voice she shouted, "Water's high, just sit steady
and you'll get through." At this moment, Pluto and his or-
der-giving, backward-looking mistress slowly and quite
decorously left the walkway and plunged into the Little
Deer Creek. And I began to re-consider the existence of a fair
and just God.

Although surprised Alice stayed composed until a few
seconds later Pluto lunged so violently that she came off and
found herself standing in thigh deep water holding Pluto's

reins. Still in control, sort of. The waiting hunt field was aghast. This could not have happened to Alice Warren, the doyenne of correct and careful hunt riding, the former District Coordinator of the Loon Hills Pony Club.

I actually felt bad for her. I could feel the freezing water seeping into her boots, the sucking clamminess of her britches, the heavy cold of her Melton frock coat, and her fingers beginning to stiffen in her very correct string gloves. Simultaneously I had to bury my face in Bosco's mane to keep from—I don't know?—laughing or crying. As Pluto and Alice scrambled up the greasy bank, her hunt cap askew and her hair net hanging off her left ear, Molly asked,

"You okay Mom?"

"Of course, no problem. It's nothing. I think the bridge has a loose plank. Go on ahead."

Molly and Boyd did just that. Possibly a cathartic moment for both? I took in the scene, the soaking disheveled Alice and a jigging Pluto, his Little Deer Creek baptism having slightly panicked him. Blood from his front left cannon bone ran down his fetlock and stained it pink. Alice was, however, determined to keep hunting.

Concerned that we were far from the trailers and vans, that a cold wind was rising, that Pluto needed first aid, that Alice was certainly in mental if not physical shock, that her core temperature was approaching hypothermia, I lied and said,

"Alice, I've got to go in early today. Dentist appointment. Let's hack back together and check Pluto's leg." She kept moving on with the hunt field.

"Really, there's a lot of blood on Pluto. I know you can't see it from the saddle but it's not pretty." This time she agreed to come with me, but not without commenting, "Really Amelia you should stay until the end of the hunt. Etiquette you know. Shouldn't schedule your appointments on possible hunt days."

Once again, I pressed my face into Bosco's mane, gave him a pat on the neck and cooed, "Nice horse, nice horse, good boy."

RONALD D. GILES

The Prey

Before sunrise, as I entered the darkness of the woods, I heard my father's voice admonishing..."*Never hunt alone.*"

At 4:30 a.m., the seldom-used logging road I was walking along looked very different than it did when I scouted the location. Yesterday, the spring canopy of leaves had provided a welcome relief from the noontime sun, but now the chilly 45-degree temperature caused me to pull the jacket hood up over my head, as I scuffled along the ruts in the darkness.

Wild turkey hunting had been forbidden in the state for twenty years, but this year the turkey population had recovered to the point that 1,000 hunters had been selected by lottery for the spring gobbler season. I was among the lucky ones, and I wasn't going to let this opportunity slip through my hands, even though I had to go alone.

As soon as I was notified of my selection, I began reading everything I could about turkeys and about how to call them using a hinged, hand-held mahogany box, the inside edges of which had to be chalked to simulate the hoarse sound of a turkey's voice.

With practice—and a lot of ribbing from my wife, Jenny—I had become proficient at the hen's call for companionship, sure to drive the gobbler wild with urgent desire. *Waaaahk, waahk. WAAAK.* Upon a return gobble from the male, another teasing, *Waahk, waaahhhk, WAAAK,* continuing the seduction until he was in shooting range.

Turkey calling is an art, but so is concealing yourself from their eyes and ears. Turkeys are reported to have telescopic eyesight and a 180-degree field of view, capable of spotting an eye blink at fifty yards. Because of this, many hunters wear black makeup on their faces and hands, and they dress in special shaggy camouflage clothes. Although I would have preferred the full gear, the expense of the clothing and makeup for this probable one-time event seemed unnecessary. I was wearing a face net with dark brown canvas coat, hat, and pants. My gun had a tight, camouflaged "sock" over the barrels to cancel the shine of gunmetal blue.

The side-by-side, 10-gauge shotgun that I carried had belonged to my dad. It took three-and-a-half-inch magnum shells, and the two barrels were choked full and extra full for long-range shooting. He had used the gun for hunting Canada Geese from blinds in cornfields.

My dad was not a successful hunter, whether for squirrels or rabbits or quail or ducks or geese. His eyes were bad, and he always seemed to catch his gun on some article of clothing, as he mounted it to his shoulder. The commotion he produced often caused the squirrel to scamper to the other side of the tree in time for the shot to miss. "Oh well," Dad compensated, "a day in the woods is better than two days at the store." Dad owned a small, neighborhood grocery store.

Once, I was sitting with Dad in a hunting blind on Mr. Jackson's cornfield when a skein of geese came into our splay of decoys. They were approaching from our left, the side where I was sitting. We rose together to fire at the birds. *Bang*, I missed; *bang,* I hit. **Boom**. Dad's shot was the loudest I had ever heard, even for the 10-gauge. I turned around and saw him sprawled on the ground.

"Dad," I asked, extending my arm to help him up, "are you all right? What happened?"

Red-faced, as he rose to his feet, he answered, "Well, that was the dadgumbest thing that's ever happened to me. Both barrels went off, almost at the same time, and knocked me on my can."

Dad had brought along his new pair of gloves. Problem was that they were work gloves — tough on the outside with thick insulation on the inside. The bulk of the gloves pressed against both triggers, and in his excitement at getting a shot, he pulled both triggers simultaneously. The combined power of two 10-gauge magnum shots forced him down.

"Let's go see how many I hit," he said with a smile. We both knew the answer.

The 10-gauge, all eleven pounds of it, is now mine. It is tiring to lug so I put a sling on it, anchored at the stock and forend; that way the gun can be carried across my back while walking distances to a blind or, in this case, into the woods. I had high hopes that the gun would be used today.

While walking to my hunting location in the darkness, I needed to be as quiet as possible, because, even at great distances, the superior hearing of the turkey could detect snapping twigs or crackling leaves. The abandoned logging road was deeply rutted, and had collected seasons of leaves in its tracks, producing, for the unwary, slippery spots and concealed noisemakers. I paid attention to the location of every step.

Through the broken clouds, pieces of moonlight mottled here and there. I was determined not to use my flashlight in the darker areas because roosting turkeys could be disturbed by an unfamiliar light. Yes, I had assured my amused wife, turkeys fly up into the trees to spend the night, protecting themselves from nocturnal predators like coyotes or wolves. However, roosting turkeys, with closed eyes, provided the perfect opportunity for determined hunters to move quietly into their domain.

At sunrise, the area would come alive with all sorts of stirring creatures, including turkeys leaving their perches for a morning feast of acorns and seeds scratched from the woodland floor. By that time, I intended to be stationed and static in place, sitting against an old oak tree, to witness their morning feeding — and their vulnerability.

The silence of the morning was crudely broken by something crashing through the underbrush to my left. I could not identify the source of the noise, except that it continued, seeming to move forward ahead of me. I must have spooked a deer. Then the sound diminished, slowing to a rustle; the noise stopped. I kept walking, relieved that it was silent again.

The sudden growl and deep bark of a dog, followed by another dog's higher yowl, chilled my spine. On the road ahead, in a grayish pool of nightlight, stood two dogs; another emerged barking from the brush...then, another. I stopped walking.

Four dogs—three bluetick-hound hunting dogs and one larger black dog—stood on the road in front of me. Their master was not in sight. The hounds were big dogs—knee high at their shoulders, crotch-high heads, long tails held upright. Two started to bark at me; the third joined in, while the fourth, the black dog, smelled the ground. Without an owner, they were a pack, relying on ancient, wolf-like instincts; these dogs were a serious danger to me.

I slid the gun off my back and broke the double barrels open. My hand was trembling as I took two red shotshells from my pocket and dropped them into the chambers, closing the gun with a *thump*. At this distance—about 25 yards—I could kill or disable all of them with the destructive buckshot spread of my two shots. If they moved any closer, though, before the buckshot spread, I would likely hit only two of them, leaving the other two dogs to maul me before I could reload.

They moved, slowly trotting my way. My mind hesitated momentarily, pausing on whether to shoot them or not; it soon became too late to shoot as the dogs began to fan out, preparing to encircle me. Nervously, I started to walk forward, saying, "Hi boys," in a friendly voice.

Keep walking forward. Even pace. Don't stop.

I had never been a dog lover, and dogs seemed to know that. When I passed papers as a kid, dogs snarled at me. My girlfriend's Chihuahua had to be put in its cage while I was in her house. As I jogged, dogs chased me until their leashes strangle-stopped them. I don't like dogs, and they don't like me.

The dogs and I kept moving, getting closer to each other. My thumb tautly pressed the safety off, then back on, checking. "Hi boys, how you doing?" They stopped barking, but kept coming.

A strong odor preceded them, a wet, sweaty-dog smell. I avoided looking directly into their eyes, fearing that it would provoke an attack. My jaw was clenched; I was determined to get through this. *Keep walking, keep walking.*

The black dog came close and went around to my right. Peripherally, I noticed that one of his eyes looked white, cloudy. I remembered seeing him yesterday, near the cross-roads where I parked. Then he had run away. This morning he was at my feet, smelling me, sniffing loudly, allowing me to pass by him. I kept walking. He followed me.

"Good boys," I said confidently, trying not to portray fear. My heart was pounding and my mouth was open, breathing in short gasps.

The second and third dogs circled to my left — tails high, not wagging. The fourth broke to my right. His ear was split, probably from a fight. The hair stood up on his back and tail ridge. It was deadly silent, except for the sounds of breathing, sniffing, and exhaling. The dogs now were all behind me, walking with me, close to me. *Keep moving. Don't run.*

One dog sneezed — not a good sign. Suddenly, I felt an open mouth and teeth graze my left boot at the calf. Then, a strong nudge on my right leg, daring me to run. Chills shivered over my body. I had to do something. Shouldering the gun, I shot high into the air over me.

BOOM.

I turned. The dogs were standing in a bunch looking at me.

BOOM. I fired high over their heads, toward the main road. The pack turned and ran, full gallop, in the direction of my shot. Buckshot rained down around me from the first shot. The dogs disappeared into the darkness.

I broke the gun open. The ejectors of the 10-gauge threw the spent shells into the brush. Quickly, I loaded two more long shotshells. *Slam.* The gun was ready again.

Was it over? I couldn't depend on that. They had run down the logging road, the way that I had come in, forcing me to keep walking deeper into the woods to get away from them.

The dogs had my smell. They could track me. No cell service here. Keep going in the opposite direction. Go to the spot you scoped out to hunt turkeys. That's the only place you know in these woods. Daylight will be better. Stay there till 11:00 a.m. when hunting is over. Move. Don't run.

Picking up the empty shells and putting them in my game bag, I threw the sling of the 10-gauge over my head and walked quickly to the dead tree, which marked my turn off the logging road. *The gun on my back was still loaded. Be careful.*

I went up the path, then over the hillside and down into the ravine between the two hills. Water was running off the hills into a small stream at the bottom of the ravine. To conceal my scent from the dogs, I walked uphill through the stream. Coming to a small pool, ankle deep, pausing momentarily to catch my breath from the uphill climb, I felt the water course over my boots. Would this lose the dogs? "Wade in the water, wade in the water, children," the old song of the Underground Railroad advised.

Stepping out of the pool, I mounted the other side of the ravine. My breathing was labored again by the eleven-pound weight of the gun. *Take a right turn at the uprooted tree stump; walk uphill to just below the ridge. There. The hunting place.*

In front of me was my oak tree with a view across another ravine. The rising sun was to my right; daylight would soon illuminate the flat spot on the other side where I had spotted the turkey scratchings yesterday. Maybe I could still hunt. Maybe the turkeys' need to eat would overcome the noise they must have heard earlier.

The dogs continued to worry me. What if they tracked me to my tree? They were still in the woods, a hunting pack of scent hounds. They could find me.

Rather than sit against the tree as planned, I decided to climb up to the first fork of the tree, to hide from the dogs. Jumping, I caught a branch and pulled myself up until my feet could help boost me further. Finally, after a small struggle, I was sitting on the wide junction of the trunk and its broad first branch. It was a hard seat, but I could see my turkey-scratching field, and I was up off the ground, away from the dogs. *My wife will have a hoot over this one,* I thought.

While donning my face net and hat, I remembered that these hunting hounds treed their prey; that was their instinct. I had just saved them the trouble; they had treed me without even being here. But...I was positive that these dogs were tracking my scent. One of them had grazed his teeth along my boot calf; he had me in his nose. Being off the ground was called for in this case, because they must be coming after me.

Sitting in a tree before sunrise, I recognized the irony of my situation—the hunter had become the hunted.

My perch was about seven feet off the ground. The dogs, standing on their hind legs, would be about five feet tall. With my feet dangling down eighteen inches, only six inches would separate me from the dogs. Not enough distance. I needed to think this through and make a plan.

Shoot first before they get to the tree—how's that for a plan? Two shots at close range—two dogs. Reload quickly, two shots—two more dogs. Problem solved. I didn't like the idea of killing them, but, should it come to that, I had no intention, at age 32, of being ripped apart by a pack of dogs. It would be them or me; I chose them.

From my roost, I could see daylight begin to show in the East; it was going to be overcast, at least for the morning. Nevertheless, I could feel the warmth of the sun penetrating the cloud cover. Bugs began flying busily about, as the muted light showed misty, foggy shapes in the hills below.

Sounds in the woods no longer echoed but were muffled, softened by the vaporous gauze in the trees.

The sky around the sun showed lavender and pinkish-orange hues, pushing in streaks through the low clouds. The colors rapidly merged, producing a brilliant red. At the sight of the reddish dawn, I heard my dad's voice again. "Red sails at night...sailor's delight," he would say in a matter-of-fact manner. Then, lowering his voice dramatically, Dad would counsel, "Red sails in the morning...sailors take warning. Son, there may be a storm coming...but not right now. Let's hunt."

I miss Dad.

The sun appeared over the horizon, radiating welcome warmth. Birds began singing and squirrels were scampering. It was time for me to join in the show.

Slowly, I removed the 10-gauge from across my back and placed the gun and sling on my lap, ready when needed. I patted the big pockets on the front of my jacket to assure myself the shotshells were still there. Two of them had been used earlier and two shells were still in my gun; six shells were left—two in the left shell pocket and four in the right one.

Now, down to business. From the inside game pocket at my back, I pulled out the hinged "Sweetness" turkey call. Taking the chalk stored in it, I liberally marked up the inside edges of the box and put the stub away in my shirt pocket. From the other shirt pocket, came my crow call. Crows are early risers, and their activity will often draw turkeys off their roost.

Blowing "caw, caw, caw," I tried to visualize a male turkey coming out of his sleep, stretching his legs, ruffling his feathers and holding his five-foot wingspan out from his sides. Bobbing his head up and down, looking side to side, the gobbler launches off his perch, flying to the ground to look for food and females.

"Caw, caw," a real crow sounded in the distance. Wait—maybe it was another hunter using his crow call. Mark the direction.

I put away the crow call and picked up the turkey call, reviewing in my mind what I was trying to simulate—the mating call of a hen turkey. Start soft, test the waters, then become insistent and confident.

"*Waaawk, waawk, waawk?*" I offered. Hopefully, that meant something like "Good morning, anybody here?"

Bugs humming...birds chirping...a woodpecker—but no turkey gobble.

"*Waaawk, waaaawak, waaaawck,*" I called more urgently.

Nothing. Only the sound of the wind blowing through the young, tender leaves.

"***Waaaawk, waaawk, WAAAAAWK,***" I insisted.

More wind through the leaves. Bugs. The woodpecker. A squirrel in the tree. Wind.

"Wobble, wobble, **WOBBLE**, **Wobble**, **wobble**, wobble," sounded in the distance. A tom answered! It was a thrilling, wild sound. Primitive. Strong.

I called again. No reply from the tom. Then a second call. Still, no answer. Chalking up my mahogany box, I tried once more. Nothing. No response from the gobbler. Maybe it was something I said...or maybe it was something I didn't say.

A chilly wind touched my face; clouds thickened in the sky. My legs began to go to sleep. Parts of my body ached from the effort of sitting in the tree junction. I moved my limbs, trying to keep quiet, afraid of scaring away a turkey, but trying to let some blood circulate.

Time passed slowly. Across the ravine, I stared at the feeding site where, in recent days, turkeys had gathered to forage. *Here turkey, turkey,* I thought. Not a turkey in sight.

If the turkeys weren't going to eat, I was: breakfast waited in my outer coat pocket. Safely stowed in a brown paper bag were two fried-egg sandwiches on buttered white bread, one for now and one for later. Surely the cholesterol of this hunter's meal would be absorbed by the adrenaline produced in the dog encounter and the efforts of hiking to, and climbing up, my tree.

Stop. I froze in place, reaching for the sandwiches. From my right, a big tom turkey, probably weighing twenty pounds, slowly entered the area. He had located my call precisely and had come to investigate. My breathing quickened.

The noises of the woods seemed to cease as the turkey deliberately stepped forward, his head moving, scanning the space. His glossy bronze tail was down, not fanned, but his wings seemed to be held slightly away from his body, in a small display, making him look bigger and more imposing. The woodland-colored feathers on his wings were iridescent, shimmering in hues of purple, red, and gold. Each strutting high step showed the sharp, dangerous spur on the back of his leg, ready to battle any other tom who might challenge him. He was magnificent.

There was no way I could raise my gun without spooking the tom. My best bet was to let him strut through, until his back was to me, and then go for the 10-gauge.

The turkey stopped. Something about his attitude changed. His feathers smoothed, his wings drew closer to his body. The tom's head stretched high into the air, looking far behind him to the right. Suddenly, he turned toward the ravine and ran quickly, his heavy wings extended. With five steps and three beats of his wings, the turkey was airborne over the break of the hill and on his way to the opposite side, dropping scat all the way. Then the tom banked right, heading down the ravine, gliding silently toward the meadow below.

In my excitement at seeing something that looked as awkward as the turkey get up and fly away, I neglected to take a shot. He was in range, but the thought of shooting never entered my mind. I patted my gun, reminding myself that it would be there and ready for the next turkey. *Fat chance.*

Why did the turkey fly? What happened? I hadn't moved. My face was veiled in camo netting, as was my gun barrel. The wind was in my face, from the North, so the tom couldn't have smelled me. What spooked him?

The answer came out of the woods to my right, the same direction as the turkey had appeared—two bluetick hounds, with their noses to the ground, padded into my clearing. I pushed the safety off my gun.

Don't move, don't shoot yourself in the leg, and don't fall out of the tree, I thought.

When the dogs found the turkey's droppings, both of them started making excited noises. Shortly, the dog with the split ear appeared; no sign of the fourth, the black dog. With the wind still in my face, the dogs had not sniffed my presence, but I caught the pungent dog-smell of them.

The three dogs mixed around each other, noses down, and then began to follow the turkey's scat over the hill to the clearing across a small ravine on the next hill. The dogs circled noisily around the turkey's scratching field, until one of them finally loped off down the hill, barking. The other two followed, howling as well, running down the hill in the direction the tom had flown. The barking receded into the distance. Relieved, I slid the safety back on.

I was glad the three dogs were gone, but their barking was ruining whatever chance I had to attract another turkey. Given all that had happened, and with the hunting prospects for the rest of the day damaged by the dogs, it seemed pointless to remain in the field. I knew where three of the dogs were; the path to my car was in the opposite direction from them. Hiking back to the car was going to be much easier, since the walking was mainly downhill and in daylight. Plus, I was just plain discouraged. Now seemed like a good time to go.

That was it: I decided to leave. Putting the sling over my head and placing the still-loaded gun across my back, I scooted down the tree and moved quickly to the left, downhill into the ravine. My senses were on high alert.

Walking along the ravine proved to be straightforward—not too steep, the water shallow. My heartbeat increased as I left the ravine and turned onto the path through the woods that led to the logging road. I didn't like hiking with a loaded gun on my back, but it was necessary. Thankfully, no dog sounds.

Reaching the logging road was a welcome relief. Soon, I would be at my car. Imagine what this climb down would have been like if I had been carrying a turkey over my shoulder. That was nothing I needed to think about now.

Jenny will be surprised to see me home earlier than expected. My hunting experience today should provide her with a lifetime of storytelling. If it wasn't so serious, it probably would be funny.

Actually, it had been a pretty amazing morning: confronted by a dangerous pack of dogs, spent the morning in a tree afraid of a dog attack, successfully called a turkey but didn't shoot when he appeared, left the field early while the dogs chased my turkey. Maybe I won't tell Jenny the whole thing right away…later…maybe later.

A dog barked from behind. Fear tightened like a vise at the sound. Without thinking, I stopped and turned around. The black dog was charging in my direction. *So, he had been tracking me!*

In a panic, I started running, then realized too late that prey on the run would only inflame the dog's instincts. The heavy gun on my back slowed my steps. I was breathing hard. *Run faster.* **Run faster.**

Just ahead was the crossroads. Through the underbrush, I could make out my Ford Explorer. Looking back, over my shoulder, I saw the dog gaining on me.

His deep, chesty "ruuuff, ruuuuff, ruuuuufff," trailed me. I fumbled for my keys. Wrong pocket! That's the sandwich bag. Right pocket. Keys. Don't drop them. Punch, punch. Brake lights; doors unlocked.

"Ruuuff, ruuuuff, ruuuuufff."

I was losing the race. He was going to get me before I could open the door. I looked back. He was twenty feet away, coming hard. I stopped by the front car door and instinctively took out the bag of sandwiches. I threw it at the black dog. The dog stopped and began sniffing the brown bag. I jerked the gun off my back.

Up the road in front of my car, the three bluetick hounds bounded from the underbrush—barking, running my way. Opening the door, I dove into the car, gun in hand, just as the three dogs raced past the car to the sandwiches. I could hear the tussling and growling of the hounds behind me, engrossed in a scrum of possession. Awkwardly, I scrambled around in the front seat and slammed the door...shut.

Exhausted, I dropped the gun on the passenger seat; it fell, barrels first into the passenger's footwell.

Safe. I was safe. Sweating and gasping for breath, my heart racing and my hands shaking...I was safe.

Looking in the side mirror, I saw the three hounds finishing the prizes they found in the brown bag; the black dog simply stood looking at my car, his mouth open, drooling.

I reached over to the other seat for my gun...to unload it. Sharp, loud scratching on the car caused me to flinch.

"Ruuufff! Ruuuuffff!" The black dog's muzzle and head were at my window. It wasn't over for him.

I sat up in the seat, my face next to his. "**RUUFFFFF**," he barked at me through the window, as he lunged up and down, smearing the window with spittle and snot, growling, clawing the door.

"Ruuuuffff! Ruuuuffff, ruuuuffff!" I started the car, meaning to drive away from him, but stopped myself. Deliberately, slowly, I turned and glared at the snarling black dog inches away, intensely fixed on his eyes, one yellow and the other cloudy. His barking halted, as we looked fiercely at each other. Stared. Stared angrily, defiantly. Stared.

The black dog eased down to the ground, moving backward to hold contact with my eyes; I held his stare. Unexpectedly, he lurched to his left, toward the road, running...then he stopped, looking back, as if inviting me to drive away so he could give chase. Quickly, I mashed the accelerator to the floor, throwing gravel. The black dog began running, but I passed him.

Driving away, I glanced in my mirror and saw the black dog hurtling after me, barking, white froth trailing out of his mouth. He wasn't giving up, still coming fast as I rounded the curve and lost sight of him.

Looking again at the road ahead of me, Dad's words echoed in my head once more: "*Never hunt alone.*"

I turned on the radio to calm myself. The announcer, in his resonant tones, was introducing the next selection…

"…with music and lyrics, written in 1937, by Robert Johnson:

'I got to keep movin', I got to keep movin'
Blues falling down like hail,
And the day keeps on remindin' me,
There's a hellhound on my trail
Hellhound on my trail,
Hellhound on my trail.' "

CHRISTINE YURICK

Sam's Brother

Lizzie looked up from the cat, sprawled on the cement, its front paw folded and curled into itself. Light trickled in through the trees and created splashes on the ground, like the water from the creek. She forgot her thoughts, the ones that pushed her on the five-mile run that she had started, and glanced back down at the cat. If the cat was here, then he couldn't be far, Lizzie thought, stood, then wiped the sweat from her brow and from the back of her neck. There were a few men fishing in the Brandywine—they stood in brown water to their waists, staring down, staring at nothing. The birds flew above, but Lizzie knew nothing of them beside the awful quietness that would come in the winter when they are gone.

The path had no flowers. Few people came to this far end of the Struble Trail. Lizzie was eager to get moving again but knew that she couldn't. She was bound to the spot in a way that she hated; bound by the memory of him, and resisting what she felt was without choice. A man passed by, walking and staring at her. She looked down. She only said hello to the women on the trail. *It was far too close to home and with my history...* her thoughts trailed off when the cat suddenly ran from her feet, into the direction that she knew and dreaded. But she also wanted. Her feet began moving.

The man walking ten yards in front of Lizzie had a large sweat mark down his back. It looked like an exclamation point. She kept her pace and still remained about the same distance behind him. He looked older, but fit and agile. His face will disappoint, she thought. Of course. She liked to keep some distance between herself and the other runners. She observed them, wondered about their hair, or clothes, or the way their muscles leaped at each step before relaxing and then exerting the pressure again. She looked down to her side, to the slow-moving water. They added fish. Parts of the creek were almost dry and other sections were a few feet deep. At one point in the trail there was a rope swing. Children would flock there after school in their bathing suits: the jocks flexing their chests as they lounged on a rock, the girls hiding behind their towels, and the others taking their turn on the swing, grabbing and letting go into the great abyss. It worried Lizzie, because the water there was too shallow. There were always kids jumping out from the edges of the path.

After Lizzie passed the laughter of the kids she realized the man she had been following was gone. She ran ahead a few yards and saw him heading up an adjacent trail to her right. She knew that trail led into the backside of the Williamsburg development. The trail up was steep and she couldn't run and catch up to him. She stopped at the bottom and watched until he reached a curve that took the path out of sight. When he reached that point, he stopped. He looked down at her in a brief glance. But one footstep more took him out of her view.

Lizzie turned around and started walking back to the path. She was sweating again. Her heart was beating fast. She walked a few paces back in the direction of home and cut off the trail on the far side, to the water, to the small island that sat between the shallow water and the rocks. She found a place under the trees and sat in the shade. Absently, she realized that she was petting a cat. The cat was dark brown with black stripes. It looked well fed.

"Where did you come from," Lizzie asked. The cat reminded her of her brother. It looked just like the one that would visit the site; she saw it whenever she went back. Why had they been driving so fast? What was the hurry?

The cat moved away and stretched out in the sun. The cat did not hurry. It is better that way, Lizzie thought as her eyes scanned her surroundings. She watched the people on the trail—the young couple running while pushing their newborn in a stroller with large wheels, teenagers talking and pedaling slowly while texting, the woman with dark hair that Lizzie passed almost every day, the older lady on the bike whose perfume smelled like cotton candy. The slight breeze that was there earlier had ended. She remembered her body and the care she put into being fit. She remembered the days of carelessness. And Tommy's warnings. Who was there to warn Tommy? No one. Not even Sam. The hot, stillness of the sun brought back the flames that she fought each day.

As Lizzie climbed back to the trail, she saw the man again, sitting on a bench. He was petting the brown and black cat. The man turned to look at her and Lizzie had the feeling that she knew that face, but not quite. Like it was familiar but different in a way. He smiled at her as Lizzie turned the other way to head home.

It was only a week ago, but Lizzie felt like it was much longer, and that she should have known who he was. But time had become foggy and increasingly unclear.

Tommy led Lizzie into the meadow and told her the names of the flowers. "It makes no difference to the flowers, what their names are," he said. When she asked him why he liked the flowers, he said, "Because they can't lie." They were kids again. They always were, when they were in the field.

As Lizzie walked the field, she let her fingertips brush against the top of the tall grass. The flowers were gone now. And so was Tommy. Her mind wouldn't accept that. She saw him everywhere—not as a ghost, but as a living memory. He wouldn't go away. He was part of her existence. As he always had been.

She reached for her phone in her pocket. She opened it to a text from Sean: "Are you stopping by?" Lizzie had forgotten. She took another look at the field. There was a small house in the distance. That was the house they grew up in. She didn't want to leave the memory. "Yes," she responded and started to walk to her car. She resisted the urge to turn around and ask Tommy to follow her.

Lizzie walked into the Taproom and said hello to the first person who recognized her. She moved this way, from person to person, around the corner of the bar. She smiled and laughed and calmed her friends who gave her a look of concern. She wanted to show them that it was unnecessary. She heard the faint gesture when they asked how she was doing.

Her eyes showed the first sign of emotion when she made her way around to Sean. He was one of her longest-standing friends. "I went to the field again." Sean looked at the archway above her head, then lowered his eyes and listened to her. "The flowers are gone." Lizzie said the same thing each time he saw her, ever since the accident. This was the first time she had been out to see friends since then. That was three months ago.

Sean had called Lizzie the day it happened. He found out from a friend but she already knew. He remembered her sobs, and the heart-wrenching silence that followed. There was an acceptance in her eyes, but the eyes were no longer the same. They would never be whole without her brother Tommy.

Lizzie left after some time that she neither enjoyed nor hated. She went home and made a cup of tea. She spent the evening as she had every night for months, with a hallow loneliness consuming her insides. As she drifted off into the nothingness, she saw the small body and honest eyes of a cat and wondered about the man who owned it.

Lizzie did not go back to the trail for two days. She couldn't remember how the time passed. One moment she was walking the field and reciting the names of flowers, and the next she was giving Tommy a hug when he was leaving the party. The smell of his cologne made her chuckle. He'd worn it since he was a little boy. Little Tommy, playing in the field. Older Tommy, getting in trouble, making friends, excelling in school. Meeting girls. Tommy in his first car as Lizzie taught him to drive stick, his sweat and determination, his angry face because she was telling him what to do. The wild times, the idle days, and then Sam. Sam the jock, the annoying punk who always said the wrong thing but who knew how to apologize; Sam the dirty kid who would come in with Tommy covered head to toe in mud and politely ask mom for a grilled cheese sandwich and some milk; Sam the boy with no fear and all the care in the world. Holding Sam's hand; holding Tommy's hand; playing together, as children, and as adults.

Lizzie ran to the door at the sound of a knock, opened it to find Sam and Tommy there, smiling, "Hurry up kid, we're gonna be late," Tommy saying, then Lizzie falling to the ground and sobbing into the empty hallway. Lizzie woke on the floor of the bedroom, holding a dead receiver to her ear, saying, "What? Tommy? What—not Tommy..." but the officer who had called that day three months ago was not on the phone. The thought of the man on the trail returned so strongly that it brought her back to reality. She dressed and went to find him. I know him; why can't I place him? She wondered and stared back at the haze of the last two days and discovered that time wasn't real anymore. It all ran together.

The trail was packed with dogs and bikes and children. Lizzie hurried through them. Maybe I should take the attention they all want to give to me right now. That can't be so wrong, can it, she accused, her eyes burning into the pavement.

Lizzie was so caught up that she ran into a man jogging in front of her. "Excuse me," she muttered without looking. Then there was a hand touching her arm and the warmth that came from the hand soothed her. Was that what the warmth in the car felt like, that burning? It drained her of any thought or emotion – at that moment, her existence simply consisted of the physical sensation of his touch. Before she could lose herself to it, she looked in his eyes.

"Lizzie," he said.

"Who are you?"

He stared at her hard. She studied his bronze skin, his half parted lips, his gray eyes, and his golden hair. He did not speak for some time.

"I'm Jerry," he drew a deep breath, "Sam's brother."

Lizzie lost another span of time. She saw, as clearly as if she had witnessed it, the odometer passing 120-mph, Sam and Tommy laughing as the darkness and breeze flew into the open windows of Sam's car, the turn and the guardrail and the endless wall of trees. Lizzie wondered about the blaze of the brilliant fire and whether they had died before the flames engulfed them. Then Jerry's hand was on her elbow and pulling her to the nearest bench. He sat next to her for what seemed like a very long time, while she stared off into some place that only she could visit.

"I forgive him," she said. "I'm so sorry..." she whispered in his ear as she held him. And she wished that she could always remain in his arms, bound together in life as their brothers were in death.

JACOB ASHER MICHAEL

As Clouds Will Always Do

Mark Berkhalter snaps a pink-flowered branch off the magnolia growing in front of the Horizons Assisted Living Center, just south of West Chester, Pennsylvania. The tree stands within twenty feet of US Route 202. The constant blasts of wind from the big rigs bound for nearby Wilmington, Delaware have so weakened each petal that they can barely keep their form. Still, they smell like the outdoors. That, Mark reckons, is just what Eleanor needs.

Eleanor Stackhouse will be the recipient of this ad hoc bouquet, and not young porcelain-skinned Becky Vilinsky. Becky has a physique not unlike the Statue of Liberty, and is prone to lay tarot cards on a table along with statuettes of fairies, archangels, and the Buddha. Eleanor, however, is a shriveled mousy-blond woman in her late fifties, whose unexplained back problems turned out to be something much worse.

Mark began visiting Eleanor the summer before, just after Becky informed him she was not ready to move in with him, in part because she was stone-cold broke and maxed out on her credit cards. And so, instead of giving Becky an arm full of springtime blossoms, or a wedding ring, Mark is strolling onto the front porch of Horizons with a few half-wilted magnolias.

This gift is not an expression of undying love. Rather it is a nice bit of nature to share with an old hippie stricken by an ancient disease cunning enough to evade all modern medical advances. Its name is ALS, and it was destroying

Eleanor's muscles while leaving her mind intact. She could ask the dean of the Harvard Medical School or some tattooed witch doctor from the jungles of Borneo, and they'd both be unable to stop it. All Eleanor's physicians could do is to give her a prescription for a slick black wheelchair that looked more like a Star Wars robot than a chair with wheels.

Like Mark, Eleanor had once lived in the Mt. Airy section of Philadelphia, with its grand stone houses and proud lesbian couples doting on their adopted inter-racial children. Just as Mark was lured into Chester County by a better paying job, so Eleanor migrated to the burbs for a tenured position at West Chester University. They both enjoyed gardening, bluegrass, and Latin jazz. Mark might have even hit on her, had she not been fifteen years older and scheduled to go into hospice.

Mark met Eleanor at Willow Branch Sangha, a small Buddhist congregation that gathered at the ultra-liberal Church of the Loving Shepherd, located in a converted stone barn down the street from the University. Eleanor attended meditation every Sunday evening for a year or so, then disappeared. This was not unusual. A lot of Buddhists are dabblers.

Nine months later, Duc Nguyn, the retired Vietnamese-born chemist from Chadds Ford who pretty much kept the sangha afloat, informed everyone that Eleanor had a fast moving form of ALS. Like everything announced at Sangha, Duc said it slowly, with a calm voice. There was no background noise, nothing for distraction. The words just sunk in. Mark accepted it as a sad reality, one of a vast multitude he was powerless to reverse.

Duc asked if anyone could help Eleanor with her physical therapy. Having no husband, children, or nearby relatives, she needed someone to move her arms and legs to break up the calcium that clogged her joints like a rusted hinge. According to Duc, she had sold her house and taken up residence in Horizons a few minutes away from Mark's office.

Based on that simple request, Mark volunteered to help. He needed to do a good deed. Becky worked in the same building he did, and every time he walked by her on the stairwell, he stared straight ahead, ignoring her very presence. It made him feel like a total jerk. Is that what a Buddhist should do? It sure didn't seem that way.

A Buddhist should be mindful, keeping things in perspective. But when Mark even glanced at Becky, he spent the next five hours cursing the fact that if they had bought a house together *as they had planned*, he would not be jumping through hoops just to get a loan for a stinking condo. And with the unfolding implosion of the mortgage industry, those hoops were looking ever more like someone had set them on fire.

There was also that buff, Teutonic New Age shaman priest Becky started dating, as well as the emergency cardiac stent surgery Mark's father just underwent. Of course, his dad's heart disease had nothing to do with Becky. Yet somehow, it fell into the mix.

These sorts of dog-chasing-its-tail thoughts are what proper Buddhists would refer to as "un-helpful." Mark had figured this out, and sought to tamp them down through charitable works, a form of active meditation as it were. Thus when Duc explained that Eleanor needed a few folks to stop by once a week, Mark went for it.

In general, if Duc suggested something, Mark did it. Duc was a methodical, organized man who had every reason to become a rich pharmaceutical company executive. Instead, he became a rich pharmaceutical company executive who hung out with the middle-class lost souls and scatterbrained oddballs who frequent American Buddhism. No doubt, his brothers back in Vietnam thought he was nuts.

Once during a Dharma Discussion at sangha, Duc told an old story about a renowned Buddhist monk who trained a young novice. For years the novice had carried his master's water and ground his ink. But the frustrated novice never felt like he was any closer to Enlightenment. One day he screamed at his master, "I work for you all day, and you don't teach me anything! I have done everything I was supposed to do."

His master pointed to a tree and said, "Look at that tree."

The novice did, and for the first time, he actually saw something.

Mark could not carry an entire tree into the small suite where Eleanor lives. But he could bring a magnolia twig. Now *that* is a very Buddhist thing to do. Whenever Thich Nhat Hahn or the Dalai Lama sit around giving a talk, there is always a little pitcher with a flower set off the side. And what is the profound spiritual significance of that flower? Probably nothing.

The leggy young woman behind the front desk at Horizons smiles. She, like most of the women who work there, is really cute. No, not just cute, hot. All that fertile beauty meandering through an antiseptic mansion populated by old ladies with swollen ankles seems like some kind of a grand metaphor. But if it is, Mark cannot fathom its meaning.

When he arrives at Eleanor's room, she is being hoisted out of her bed by a seriously large pudgy African. He holds her in a bear hug with his arms underneath hers, and lowers her into her wheel chair. She fiddles with the toggle switches on her armrest, adjusting the padded crescent roll supporting the back of her head.

"Thank you, Linwood," she says, as if huffing the thin air on the plains of Tibet. Her accent is that of northern Virginia's gentry, tempered by a Ph.D. in education from Temple University.

Linwood silently plods out the door, nodding toward Mark as he passes.

Mark knocks on the door jamb. Eleanor pilots her chair around.

"Linwood is a dancer," she says. "The first time he picked me up, he held me in a tango hold."

"Do you dance tango?"

"I took classes years ago." She points her curled fingers toward a bookcase. "Could you grab those checks? I need you to write some for me."

Mark rips out two checks. She tells him what to write. One will transfer thousands of dollars into an account. It dawns on him how easily someone could defraud her.

She asks, "How is the house coming along?"

"Good, I think. The mortgage guy mailed some papers for me to sign, but he sent them to the condo I am buying rather than the apartment where I *actually live*. He does some pretty stupid things. I had to keep phoning him from the hospital where my dad is staying. It was a mess."

"You will be so happy when you're in your own place. Paperwork is always a drag. There are some stamps in the drawer of my nightstand. Could you put them on the envelopes?"

Atop the nightstand rests a bank envelope and the final electricity bill from her old house. Mark stamps them.

Eleanor says, "Sign them and seal them up."

"The checks? You want me to sign these?"

"Don't worry. My handwriting is illegible. No one will care."

He signs them.

Eleanor rolls out of her cramped room and into the perpetually empty hallway where she and Mark always do her exercises. It is a clean and pleasant space. Too clean actually, like a nice hotel, not a place where you live. On the walls are pictures of Victorian women on swings. The ceilings are broken with skylights to give the shut-ins a dose of daylight. Mark pushes a loveseat off to the side so he can better move around.

Then he holds onto Eleanor's foot, raising it up and down fifteen times to get the ankle moving. First the right, then the left. He says, "I may be going to Hawaii next year. My cousin just moved out there. I figure I can sleep on his couch and go out while he's at work. They have a ukulele festival not far from his house. That would be the real deal."

"That sounds great. I went to a Maori dance contest in New Zealand once. Are you close with your family?"

"With my sisters, yes. I have thirty two cousins. I only know a handful of them."

"I have a hundred cousins. Or at least I used to. Some of them died."

"A hundred? How many aunts and uncles do you have?"

"My mother had eight siblings. My father had fourteen. One of my aunts is a year younger than me. We went to elementary school together. Let's do the knees."

Mark pulls her foot up by the heel. The initial lift is no challenge, but getting her leg straight is like closing an overstuffed suitcase.

She lets out a guttural sigh and says, "I am trying to memorize the Five Remembrances. You want to hear them?"

"Sure."

"*I am of the nature to grow old. There is no way to escape growing old. I am of the nature to have ill health. There is no way to escape ill health. I am of the nature to die. There is no way to escape death. All that is dear to me and everyone I love are of the nature to change. There is no way to escape being separated from them. My actions are...* oh, crap. What's the fifth one?"

Mark focuses on her other leg. It is much easier than looking her straight in the face. If he makes eye contact with her he might break into tears and look like a fool. That would just bring her down. He couldn't do that.

Instead he says, "I don't know that sutra," and again his mind wanders.

He realizes that Eleanor, withered and weak, is not just yapping out some silly old chant. She is living it. Over the years, Mark had been to all kinds of seminars about Buddhist thought and practice. They were full of deep, mind-as-a-mirror concepts, but this is not theory. She is actually, genuinely, really *not* going to escape death. Her light switch has been turned off. It is just a matter of time till the bulb goes out.

"Why," says Mark, "are you memorizing it?

"It gives me comfort. I heard that the mon
Village chant it every night before they go to sleep

Mark continues pushing her heel forward ⌐uck,
wondering how that god-awful depressing chant could ever
give anyone comfort. They chant *that* before they sleep? If
anything, it is a recipe for nightmares. And yet, if Eleanor, in
the shape she is in, says that it does her good, who is Mark
to argue?

Eleanor flicks the joystick on her armrest so that she is
lying face up. The motherly electrical hands of her wheelchair cradle her like an infant, supporting her legs, butt, and
head.

Mark moves her wrist. Up, down Up, down.

Eleanor peers at the skylight directly above her.

She asks, "Are you still doing yoga?"

"Not much. I've been super busy at work since my boss
died, and I have to cart my mom all over the place until my
dad gets better. She can drive around the neighborhood, but
she gets flustered on the highway."

"Yoga is a smart thing to do. You should get back into
it. Are you going to meditation?"

"No. Becky shows up there with her boyfriend and I just
get angry. There's a meditation place over in Havertown. I
might try going there."

Eleanor asks, "You ever been married?"

"No."

"I was once. You should never get married." She adds,
"That's enough. Do the elbow."

Mark's only response is to pump her forearm back and
forth. After all, what is he supposed to say? He had all but
given up on ever finding love. Then Becky wandered into
his life offering opportunities for hope and a future, not to
mention sex and someone to talk to. Or was it just a hor-
mone-induced lapse in judgment? Becky was clueless about
who she was. The fact that she hid so much from Mark
wasn't nearly as bad as all the stuff she hid from herself.

If only she had told Mark about her debts. She spent
months roaming around Media Borough looking at houses

with him. Was she just playing along? And now he has to call the moron from the bank about APRs and loan-to-value ratios from the hospital waiting room, all because County-wide Mortgage went bankrupt and everyone at the real-estate office freaked out. This deal left him with only $3,000 in his account. What if the heater breaks down? What if his twelve-year-old Subaru explodes?

Then, through the roaring tsunami of his ruminations, Mark hears Eleanor's voice.

Almost like a little girl, she says, "Look at that cloud!"

With that, the typhoon in Mark's mind stops. He recalls Duc's story of the novice screaming, "I've done everything I was supposed to do." Like in an automobile accident, time slows down.

Mark lets go of her arm. He gazes toward the skylight.

Eleanor has just directed him to look at that cloud, and if she says so, he must do it. Even if it kills him right there, he has to look. Keeping his eyes wide open, he raises his head, noticing every bone in his neck curving into an arc.

He sees a blue sky, through which floats a white cloud. At that moment, he knows exactly what he is doing. He is looking at a cloud.

He doesn't feel good or bad, or scared or abandoned. The experience does not cure him of his ills. There is no magical experience or dynamic flow of transcendent light energy. All that stuff's just bunk.

But something does happen. If only for a couple of minutes, the Practice generates results the way it's supposed to, the way the Buddha said it would some two thousand years ago.

Mark remains still, doing just what his Zen master has instructed him to do. With his mind more steady than it has been for weeks, he sees the cloud glide through the window pane, a scene as surreal as any painting by Magritte.

Eleanor sees it too.

And then, with the two of them staring at the sky from within a building, the cloud slowly drifts away, as clouds will always do.

PETER CUNNIFFE

An Incident Near Paoli

18 September 2009

Chas,

Your letters from Afghanistan have all reached me. My apologies for not having written sooner. I'd bitch and moan about the pain of relocating before senior year of high school, but I know any tale of woe would pale next to yours — a point that Mom rubs in my face at every opportunity. Besides, it may not end so badly.

Here is an inventory of what I lost in my most recent transition:
> *The first real girlfriend I ever had*
> *Four true friends*
> *My spot on the varsity soccer team*
> *The nickname "Dunfer" - a name that proved only slightly more palatable when pronounced with our New England disdain for the final 'r' sound ("Hey, dun'FAH!")*

Here is an inventory of what I gained:
> *Dad's '98 Volvo - intended to soften the blow of leaving Concord HS*
> *An authentic Revolutionary War uniform, Black Irish style, 2nd Pennsylvania Regiment, complete with musket and bayonet - an attempt by Dad to sell me on the regional history in order to keep my Harvard plans alive*

A super-sized room in a sterile community of suburban McMansions
A seat in an exclusive suburban prep school
Weekends of being left alone to explore the lush history of the Brandywine Valley and City of Brotherly Love
The hope that Mom just might start smiling again

The school is no easier or harder than in Massachusetts, just smaller. And — get this — all boys! There are several all girl schools in the area, but I don't see myself making too much effort toward seeking them out. "One and done" - that's my motto here. Dad's wicked pissed that I didn't at least try out for the soccer team, but, I mean, come on! These guys have been playing together for three years, and I'm gonna strut onto the field and make an impact. Not likely. I'd rather lay low, and get out of here as soon as possible. Dad says he understands, but thinks soccer would make my time go quicker. No thanks.

Cliques abound here. I've been relegated to the senior's cafeteria section mockingly called "Cipher's Corner." Five other kids and me all grouped together by default — none of us jocks, trust fund jerks, or even nerds, the latter classification warranting three full tables across the linoleum-tiled room. Our crime: being ordinary kids. I know my excuse, but cannot imagine how the others made it to senior year without having formed some sort of deeper relationships. Two of these loners have tried to befriend me. It seems a last ditch effort by each of them, a daily peppering of questions directed at me from my left and another from my right. I am half surprised, half impressed with their persistence in the matter. Why is it they had never latched onto someone else, or at least each other, before I was introduced to their table? Wayne DiAntonio is tall and gangly, blemished by red and raised acne and an unruly head of wiry brown hair. He seems genuinely interested in the geographical importance of his region as related by me over dry burgers and greasy fries. Marc Norris, short with a high-pitched voice and a blonde crew-cut, likes to agree with my analysis, but otherwise rarely offers more than an occasional question to the conversational mix.

Dad was right about the history. Once our (his) decision to move was finalized, I changed my focus from "the shot heard around the world" to the events leading up to the encampment at Valley Forge, the winter that made King George understand the futility of trying to maintain the colonization of this new world. Much to learn and explore. This much I've learned already: my prep school sits — literally — on top of the Paoli Massacre site. How cool is that? I've borrowed a couple of books on the topic from the library. After my schoolwork is finished, I read my nights away and plot weekend jaunts to the various sites I've read about in the books.

One and done, bro! One and done.

-Dunc

At Wayne's sheepish urging, Duncan escorted both Wayne and Marc to Brandywine Battlefield one Saturday morning. He offered that he was going, and they both expressed interest. They walked the lines, Duncan pointing to the names and locations of brigades, both British and Continental. He spun slow circles pointing out the location of arrival and departure for both armies, acknowledging landmarks — rivers, hills and valleys, some of which could not even be seen. He set the stage for the Brandywine showdown in drawn out detail for Marc, who must have asked a hundred questions, each time expressing amazement that Duncan actually knew the answer. Wayne, more quiet than usual, absorbed it all. Duncan went about exploring that which he had set out to explore, counting in measured strides the distance between lines and pickets, discovering, to his surprise, that their naïve questions actually helped him formulate more detailed analysis, helped him better understand the geography and history of independence.

The three trod the battlefield at Brandywine for three full hours, after which they wended their way north along the Brandywine River in Duncan's Volvo until they reached West Chester, Wayne and Marc now referring to the city only as "Turk's Head" upon learning its historic name. The three talked history, or more appropriately — Duncan talked history and the other two soaked it in. He was as amazed by how little they knew about American history as they were amazed by how much he did. Over lunch at Penn's Table, Duncan presented a crash course on topics ranging from Lexington to liberty. He shared his life-long attraction with the American Revolution, the way a teen might detail his childhood love of baseball or Pokemon. Also over lunch, and also at Wayne's urging, Duncan offered to accompany — as well as drive — the two of them to the homecoming football game the next Saturday.

Though Duncan had no love of football and no desire to attend the game, he had formed a bond with Wayne and Marc. He found them amusing, even likeable. This game also provided him the opportunity to see local legend, fellow senior, and big-man-on-campus, Sean McCaffrey, demonstrate the football prowess that had earned him his big-shot reputation. The same reputation that had him listed as an all-American candidate and a recruiting prospect for the top college football programs in the country. Until this night, Sean McCaffrey, *Caff* to his doppelgangers, was nothing more than a chiseled blonde head on a size eighteen neck protruding from the bland prep school uniform. A figure known to Duncan for laughing at his own jokes, accepting (and expecting) the adoration of those around him, faculty included, and ignoring questions directed toward him by his classroom teachers. The Daily Local recently wrote an article about the football star and his soon-to-be-realized dream of playing linebacker for Notre Dame. Duncan's mother clipped the piece for her son and acted as excited as if she had known Sean McCaffrey personally. "Look, Duncan," she beamed, "an all-star, like Charlie, this boy from your school." Duncan forced a smile and informed his mother that he was going to attend the homecoming game with a couple of friends from school.

Duncan heard his own voice cheering on the team, swept up in the moment lemming-style. Wayne enjoyed peppering the opposition, the refs, the coaches, a water boy who had slipped on the muddy field, even the cheerleaders on occasion. Marc hollered along, a one-second lag on everything Wayne shouted. If Duncan didn't know the two, he would have found them annoying. He was certain many near them did. Because he knew them, he chuckled softly at their antics. The opposition was a pushover, trailing by thirty points at the half. The trio strolled beneath the grandstands at halftime with unfulfilled designs on meeting girls from the sister school up the road, girls probably waiting by the locker room for a glimpse of Sean McCaffrey.

Late in the third quarter with his team leading by a score of forty-nine to three, Sean McCaffrey was called for holding while dropping back in pass coverage on a third-and-long play for the opposing offense. Despite the lopsided score, the linebacker argued with the referee who threw the flag, and proceeded to get ejected from the game. To Duncan's amusement, the player continued his rant on the sideline, smashing his helmet to the ground and shoving aside his more rational teammates. Duncan, in a low voice, questioned whether an outburst of the sort in a blowout game was the result of steroid-induced rage. Wayne and Marc didn't answer him directly; rather, both began chanting loudly in the direction of their almost famous linebacker, "Roid Rage! Roid Rage! Roid Rage!"

The resulting scuffle was initiated by a man two rows behind the boys — as it turns out, Sean McCaffrey's father. "Youze sons of bitches!" he shouted, grabbing both of them by the collar of their jackets and pushing aside the patrons in the row separating the boys from the man. "Take it back, youze sons of bitches." The steamy waft of whiskey accompanied each syllable. He was shaking them hard, catching the attention of all around them including, fortunately, two uniformed officers and, unfortunately, Sean McCaffrey, himself. "My son don't take no drugs," he barked, as the two tried to squirm away. "Take it back."

Duncan acted in defense of his new friends. He jerked Wayne free using the front of his friend's jacket, then did the same for Marc. Facing the man, he offered calmly, "Apologies, sir. We were mistaken. It is obvious your son comes by his anger-management issues honestly." This comment incited laughter from several adults around the melee, including one of the now-present officers. The officer suggested the boys relocate, a suggestion Duncan heartily embraced.

As the three clunked down the steel bleachers, the elder McCaffrey could be heard shouting, "See those three, Sean? See 'em? You oughta kick their asses." This suggestion elicited moans from all adults within earshot. Sean McCaffrey, separated by a chain-link fence and a three-foot hedge, silently stared down the three classmates.

9 October, 2009

Chas,

I am sitting in the shade of a pagoda at Battle of the Clouds Park. I don't write you for a lifetime, then — boom! — two letters in two weeks. I thought you'd appreciate the fruits of my historical labor, though.

General Howe and the British troops kicked some serious Continental butt at Brandywine. Howe's forces gave spirited chase as far as Turk's Head, but inexplicably let the revolutionaries retreat with only the occasional musket charge from Hessian Jagers. The Continentals were disorganized and hasty in retreat, fearing their cause all but lost. If Howe had pressed from Turk's Head, it might well have been. The Continental Army was ordered to halt in the valley our Welsh brethren named Duffryn Mawr, The Great Valley, near a tavern called the White Horse. They were trudging toward a crossing known as Matson's Ford, where it was expected that General Howe would attempt a crossing into Philadelphia — an event that would almost certainly dissolve the revolutionaries' aspirations of freedom.

Continental artillery were rallied at a place called Bacton Hill. General Howe's troops advanced, intent on ending the revolution for good. Pickets were established and various orders undertaken to prepare for battle that next day. With the morning light, final preparations occurred. Cannons were placed. Powder unkegged. Muskets loaded. Lines formed. All the while, Howe's dragoons and grenadiers paced the hill making their own preparations — red coats a-scurry amid the less bold hues of autumn. As final orders were being commanded a most unexpected thing happened. Out of the south swept a terrible line of dark clouds, "more purple and green than gray" to relate a soldier's correspondence. The letter-writer thought it a harbinger signaling our fledgling nation's eminent defeat at the hands of the British. This soldier's words best paint the mood of the Continentals that day: "The clouds unleashed a burst more violent than any army could ever put forth. Men and powder soaked before cover could be sought. The British took retreat, as did our Continentals. We encamped safely that night after the long, muddy trudge to Yellow Springs, heaving our baggage up the steep north mountainside. Of what comes next am I uncertain. Gen. Howe senses our tenuous position. I am reminded, however, that Providence holds sway in the outcome. This thought keeps me moving onward, hopefully toward the cause which inspires such sufferings — that of freedom."

More to come, bro...

-Dunc

Sean McCaffrey closed in on the table as soon as they started their Monday lunch. "Three-fifteen. Top of the hill, by the statue. All three of you." It wasn't a question.

"Let me *talk* to him," Duncan pleaded as they traversed the hill, sensing Wayne actually wanted to fight.

Sean McCaffrey was perched atop the hill amid the autumn-tanned trees, and a statue, ironically, of Jesus Christ, arms outstretched in loving invite. Three lackeys were laughing at comments being swallowed by the wind. McCaffrey, obviously, had his agenda mapped out. "I want you two pussies," he snarled, pointing at Wayne and Marc, "to have the pleasure of watching me kick Ferrick's ass."

"I don't want to fight, Sean."

"Should have thought of that before insulting my old man."

"He was hurting them."

"Cause they were saying stupid shit that they shouldn't have been saying. Now put 'em up."

"I'm not fighting."

"C'mon. Don't make me knock you cold while you're just standing there," he begged with a laugh. Three voices roared in amusement over his shoulder.

Duncan was ready to be dropped cold if that was required. Live to face another day, he figured.

One of the muscles interjected, "Trouble, Caff!" pointing to a Jeep racing up the grass hill. All seven boys turned. Duncan recognized the Jeep of his math teacher, Mr. Flood.

The Jeep stopped hard beside the boys, tearing up a patch of wet grass. "Not a fight up here, is there boys?"

"He insulted my dad," started Sean McCaffrey, as if he might be given permission based on this information. "In front of a hundred strangers, no less."

"But..." Mr. Flood paused, meaningfully, "there's not going to be a fight up here, is there boys?"

"No, sir." responded Sean McCaffrey.

"Because if there are any fights on campus, Mr. McCaffrey, I assure you, you will be suspended from the football team."

Sean McCaffrey didn't bother to hear the teacher out. "Watch your back, Ferrick," he mumbled. McCaffrey strode immediately down the hill, three cohorts and a wake of ire on his heels.

Mr. Flood shook his head slowly. Turning his attention back to the others, he asked, "Anything you boys would like to talk about?" Nobody spoke. "Nothing at all?" After Sean McCaffrey was back in the school building, Mr. Flood eased into low gear and rolled down the hill.

"We would've pummeled him," offered Wayne seriously. Duncan sighed.

17 October, 2009

Chas,

Muddy roads proved to be the least of the Continental troubles. General Washington was dealt a tough decision: fall back to Matson's Ford in an attempt to prevent Howe from crossing the Schuylkill there and walking into the cradle of liberty — Philadelphia, or protect several key resources: the foundries to the west at Lancaster and the north at Reading. Washington's choice to protect the foundries had the founding fathers seeing red; not to mention packing for the relative safety of Trenton. The Continentals pushed north, giving General Howe's British Army a straight eastward shot over the Lancaster Pike toward Philadelphia. Howe took this path, but, perplexingly, eased his pace. When Washington's scouts reported the leisurely pace, Washington commanded General "Mad" Anthony Wayne to double back behind the British. He hoped to pin King George's troops front and rear at the crossing.

Howe realized his blunder too late. Washington had outflanked Howe by reaching the ford on his north-to-east-to-south course. When word reached Howe that Wayne's troops were camped near Paoli, he knew that he had squandered any advantage gained at Brandywine. Two armies and a strong river deprived him a path of retreat. His response? Howe's troops (specifically those led by a General Grey) pressed against Gen. Wayne's battalions in what correspondence calls 'a manner most savage' near Paoli. Under cover of darkness and with neither warning nor powder did they march into Wayne's encampment felling wigwams and spearing any and all, despite calls for quarters, or surrender in our current vernacular. Wayne's Continentals were slaughtered mercilessly that night. The unannounced and ruthless engagement was unprecedented. The British soldiers, backs to the wall, had responded brutally. Wayne, depending on which version of the facts one reads, either froze, allowing Continentals to be speared without structured engagement, or urged hasty retreat. Injured and escaping Revolutionaries withdrew to the Friends Meeting House at Uwchlan, once again tipping the war in Howe's favor.

This place is crawling with history, bro.

-Dunc

Turns out Wayne was acquainted with a couple of girls from the sister school, one of whom, if not invited him, made him aware of a party in the Shadow Oaks neighborhood two Saturdays later; a girl whose parents were vacationing in San Francisco and leaving their trusted daughter home alone. "*Of course* you two are invited," he promised over lunch. It was a small thing, he told Duncan. Marc echoed this point. Not for the "in crowd." Again, the echo. The unspoken translation was, of course, Sean McCaffrey would not be in attendance. "Besides," Wayne offered after a moment's silence, "the football team is playing in Maryland that day." Despite his misgivings, Duncan agreed.

Wayne's estimation of the party prevailed. It wasn't actually a small thing, but it wasn't the weekend meeting point for the in crowd either. "Nerd central," Wayne whispered with no recognition that he was welcome there. Duncan enjoyed this social setting, as it let him expand beyond Wayne and Marc. He might fit in despite his lack of effort in that regard. Several of the girls were admittedly taken with his New England accent, and, maybe, the quiet confidence that he held as his trademark. He left the duo in the basement by the pool table, and struck up a deeper conversation with a girl named Leslie. She attended Tredyffrin High School, and though she repeatedly mocked his prep-school pedigree, she seemed to enjoy his company. All was going well for Duncan. Until the rumor spread: *Sean McCaffrey is here.* Duncan looked back at his friends and caught the panic in their eyes. "I'll be right back," he informed Leslie and cut quickly to Wayne and Marc.

"Let's run for it," Marc said.

"We can't spend forever on our heels, Marc. Besides, he won't start a fight in someone's house. Wait here. I'll go talk to him." A hand gesture as he ascended the basement stairs, two palms slowly down, urged Wayne and Marc to relax.

Upstairs, he sought out the All-American. While he failed in this mission, he did spy a number of football jerseys circulating the upstairs rooms, one of whom he recognized from atop the hill when McCaffrey attempted to fight him. After several laps of the main floor, Duncan grew uneasy. He headed for the basement, but was immediately cut off by jersey number 68. "Hello, Ferrick!" the voice offered jovially, a handshake engaging a too-tight grip. The hand did not release his.

"I'm trying to go downstairs."

"No you're not."

Duncan sensed the futility. "You're right. Sorry." He backed away and the hand released his.

At the front door, Duncan found two more jerseys waiting. "Hey, Ferrick," said one of McCaffrey's minions. The kitchen door and garage door provided the same type of greeting. Duncan was trapped.

A crowd amassed by the rear dining room's bay window; murmurs and stifled screams from the party-goers. Duncan didn't need to push forward to know what was transpiring. Later in the evening, Marc related the episode in gory detail.

Panicked, Wayne and Marc slipped out the basement door. Of course, Sean McCaffrey was waiting for them.

Wayne nodded at the linebacker. "Let's do this," he stated flatly. Marc tugged at Wayne, as if to pull him back in the house, but his lanky friend shrugged him off. Wayne jumped into a boxer's stance of the sort portrayed in a Bug's Bunny cartoon.

Sean McCaffrey burst into laughter. "Holy shit! Are you serious?"

"Come on, McCaffrey. You're a second-rate player on a third-rate team, so live big now, loser. Here's your chance."

Wayne lasted two punches before his knees buckled. A spurt of red poured from his nose as he dropped. It should have ended right there. But it didn't. Sean McCaffrey, looking squarely into Marc's worried eyes, pulled Wayne up into a sitting position and proceeded to pound his face with hard rights. Three, four, five. Violent thuds accompanied the unnatural twists and drops of Wayne's head. Torrents of blood. Sean McCaffrey smirked, his eyes meeting Marc's after each punch. Finally taking his cue, Marc charged, a high-pitched scream his battle cry. He didn't even see the punch. Only the calming blackness.

"This party sucks, boys!" Sean McCaffrey shouted to the night sky. All of the jerseys made for the front door.

"You're next," whispered a stranger in Duncan's ear.

5 November 2009

Chas,

After the incident near Paoli, General Washington felt compelled to surrender Matson's Ford, leaving the City of Brotherly Love to General Howe and his red-coated army. Washington and the remnants of Wayne's troops (including Wayne, himself) fell back to Camp Towamencin, north of Philadelphia. The signers of the Declaration of Independence were fuming at Washington's mismanagement of the war, contemplating his immediate replacement. The Continentals were left licking their wounds, while the British Army prepared for a comfortable winter in the city proper. General Wayne, for his own part, declared court martial – get this, bro – against himself. Himself! He insisted that he be tried in order to prove his own innocence in the incident that had so damaged the Revolutionary cause. Washington sat in judgment, and after the calling of several witness and Wayne's defense of self, Mad Anthony was declared innocent of all charges, his standing in the Continental Army intact.

Washington ordered a detachment from Conway's 6th Pennsylvania Regiment to attack the British outpost at Beggarstown. He seemed more driven to convince his own financiers that the cause was not lost than intent on serving His Majesty notice that Continental designs on freedom had not yet waned. Vedettes had informed the Commander of a two-mile space between the main of the British troops and the Beggarstown picket. Without designs on reclaiming Philadelphia, the mission objective was to wreak havoc on the post, possibly drawing the British troops away from the city.

Along the fog-coated Germantown road, men rattled saber and bayonet, taking turn in inspired voice of shouting "Remember the incident near Paoli" and "Avenge Wayne" and "No quarters." Unbridled hatred was evident in the Revolutionary troops. The clash itself proved less an event than the march, though it is true that quarters were not always shown the enemy at the attack on the home of a loyalist by the name Allen where the British infantry sought refuge. The excursion ended in a relaxed retreat, the Continental message having been satisfactorily served.

'til next time, bro.

-Dunc

Four days later, his jaw too sore to speak, Wayne made his request in writing. "Teach us about Valley Forge, Dunc." Duncan half expected the double-black-eyed Marc to parrot in writing, but his high-pitched and now too nasal voice piped up, "Yeah, Dunc. Valley Forge." Duncan retrieved the two of them, but before the Valley Forge tour Duncan drove them from the site of the Towamencin Camp down Germantown Pike to the Allen house. On the way he related tales of the bubbling hatred in the Continental troops, the vengeance-fueled forage made on the Beggarstown Picket.

Duncan sidled the Schuylkill from Germantown back out to Valley Forge and pulled into the General Varnum picnic area with his two friends. In the empty parking lot, Duncan popped his trunk to show them the bayonet his father had gifted him when the decision was made to move to the area. Next, at a picnic table, Duncan laid out his plan. Marc was rubbing his hand up and down the nicked gray bayonet in a way that alarmed Duncan. He pulled it back away from his friend. "My father bought me an authentic uniform, Black Irish style, 2nd Pennsylvania Regiment. The musket doesn't work, except to mount the bayonet." Wayne was flipping the pointed steel over in his hands now, trying to inspect it with his one good eye. "Just to scare him, see. A little saber rattling is all. Anyhow, tomorrow at lunch you both need to let me know if you are in. If we don't do this Monday, it isn't going to happen."

"Oh, we're in," Marc insisted. "We're in."

Wayne nodded his head in agreement.

"Monday at lunch. Just nod is all. Sleep on it." He placed the weapon back in his trunk and climbed back in the Volvo. "The Valley Forge section of today's history lesson will have to wait. I just want to get home." Without further word, they walked to the Volvo.

Lunchtime Monday passed without a word, only two solemn nods followed by a third. Occasional laughter and French fries flew in from the football tables.

"Jesus Christ, Norris! You wore hunter orange to a goddamned covert operation," mumbled Wayne.

"Don't worry, Wayne" interjected Duncan. "He won't even see you two if you do everything right."

"It was cold this morning," offered Marc weakly.

"Don't worry. All you two need to worry about is pulling the tripwire at the right time. Got it?"

The three of them were at the edge of the parking lot, Duncan's Volvo resting in the space next to Sean McCaffrey's Mustang.

"Can I see it again?" asked Marc.

"No. And be quiet. He can't know anyone else is here when he sees me, or else it won't work."

Duncan sat about fifteen feet up the hill, facing back toward the school. Marc and Wayne squatted by the hoods of the Volvo (Wayne) and the Mustang (Marc). Dusk was inching into Great Valley by the time this particular late-September football practice ended and the players made for home. Sean McCaffrey held two players at his heels, just as Duncan anticipated. He recognized the figure at about twenty feet from the Mustang.

"Ferrick? What the hell you doing?"

In a move he practiced mentally about a hundred times since he settled on the hill, Duncan turned his head aside, spit into the grass casually, and stated, "Figured I'd come to you. Counter your tendency for sneak attacks." He stood on the hill as the football star dropped his backpack on the trunk of his car.

"All right then." Sean McCaffrey laughed. "Let's finish this." He walked between the two cars, his lackeys staying behind him but smiling as if glad to be at the event.

Matching Duncan's cool, McCaffrey began to say, "You've got balls, Fer—" when he stumbled to the ground. Before he knew what was happening, Duncan had spun the athlete onto his back and plopped himself knees-first across Sean McCaffrey's torso. Duncan, with a white-knuckled right hand, forced the bayonet upward and into his enemy's neck. Hard, too. Not deep, but enough to let Sean McCaffrey know he was for real. A trickle of red raced from where the steel touched skin and slid toward the ground. Duncan heard movement behind him. Both Wayne and Marc appeared on his periphery, and Sean McCaffrey's teammates moved around in front of Duncan. He smirked at their tactical clueless-ness.

"Now listen to me," Duncan began.

"Shit, Ferrick. Let up on the—"

"Shut up!" Duncan put more pressure on the bayonet. Either the force in his tone or the wild look in his eyes informed Sean McCaffrey that he had something to fear. "You try to maneuver out of this or even flinch, my first move will be to drive this thing deep into your neck. Hear me?" Sean McCaffrey said nothing. "You hear me?" Duncan exerted more force onto the spear.

"Yeah," whimpered Sean McCaffrey.

"Either of your friends move toward me, I do the same. I'm past the point of caring. Got it?"

"Yeah." That Sean McCaffrey had lost his considerable cool was evident in his shaky voice.

"Good." Duncan's voice relaxed, though the fixed look in his eye and the flex of his arm carried continued tension. "Because I need to tell you something about escalating violence, something about history. So listen up."

"Right here, maybe on the very spot we occupy, Continental soldiers begged for their lives at the hands of the 2nd Battalion of Light Infantry under the direction of British Major General Charles Grey. Just over two-hundred-and-thirty-two years ago. It was a horrible and horribly uncivilized attack that came to be known as the Paoli Massacre."

"Ferrick, I—"

"Shut up. Shut up!" Spittle sprayed the prone football player. "Even those sympathetic to the Crown believed it a cowardly and ungentlemanly affair. The British didn't even have powder in their guns. They were ordered to remove their flintlocks, to ensure they couldn't fire in the event of resistance and alert the enemy of their stealth movement. It was all bayonets and hatred on that night. And despite calls for mercy, Continental soldiers were stabbed repeatedly even as they tried to escape."

Sean McCaffrey started sobbing. "Ferrick, just—"

"And musicians. One drummer killed and at least two other musicians run through that vicious night. Did you know that musicians were considered protected in warfare before that night?" The wildness in Duncan was increasing. The fear in Sean McCaffrey kept pace. The four spectators were enraptured by the most passionate history lesson they ever experienced. "Did you?"

"No," offered Sean McCaffrey through tears.

"Well they were. But that isn't what I wanted to tell you about. What I really want to tell you about is the Battle of Germantown. I'll bet you're not familiar with that one either. It transpired about two weeks after the Paoli Massacre. October 4, 1777. A week of cat-and-mouse between Howe and Washington ended with the British taking Philadelphia without so much as a scuffle. Can you believe that?"

"No." Sean McCaffrey knew, based on Duncan's inflection, to answer.

"Neither could the Continental Congress. They had to run for their lives. Washington ordered Conway's Pennsylvanians to test the outpost at Germantown Road, maybe to appease the parties seeking his resignation. But here is what I need you to know: the Continentals significantly outnumbered the picket that Howe left behind at Germantown. The picket had no more chance than the Continentals did here two weeks earlier. The troops were rallied into battle by the cry of 'Remember the incident near Paoli.' Picture it: Continental soldiers, volunteers for the cause of freedom, themselves the victim of a merciless attack, bearing down on the outnumbered British advance guard. Thoughts of hatred filled their once-proud heads, thoughts of vengeance, of attack without mercy, without quarters. Despite the wrongness of it all. Imagine the thoughts that must have been racing through their minds just as they broke into their battle charge. Can you, McCaffrey? Can you?"

Sean McCaffrey could only cry. His eyes were shut tightly, and the bobbing that accompanied his sobs pressed the bayonet tighter into his neck, red streams running in several directions now. Duncan Ferrick had achieved everything he had set out to accomplish. He sensed the dryness in his mouth, felt the sticky bubbles at the corners of his lips, felt his arm relaxing.

What unfolded next, Duncan can only recall in swirls of slow-motion color. A blur of orange from his right controlling his arm, directing the bayonet point. A shrill cry. Duncan's own arm and weapon being thrust deep into Sean McCaffrey's neck. A gurgle, a twitch, a warm red spray splattering his face, assaulting his mouth and nose. Marc Norris kneeling beside him. "Oh, shit. Oh, shit!" falling from Wayne's mouth. Two voices shouting for their coach, fading into the distance. His own chest pounding, ringing in his ears. Adult voices. Bright lights. Marc's mantra of *I'll take the fall* repeating incessantly. Flashing red and blue lights. Handcuffs. Questions. A stretcher. Voices of long ago begging for quarters. Screams piercing the night. A car door slamming, worlds of long ago being shut away. And still Marc's chirpy (and now stoic) voice requesting the blame. All of the blame. But Duncan knew, knew too well, there was enough to go around.

12 February 2010

Chas,

Imagine the emotional state of the average Continental soldier — ragged, underfed, underpaid, having lived on the cusp of defeat, victory, and defeat again, having been ambushed in the night, shown no mercy when mercy was his plea, flipping between faith in Providence and the despair of battle, feeling a part of something important, of something doomed. Being relegated to what? Waiting. Simply waiting. The cold was no more a deterrent than was the King of Prussia's gift of General Von Steuben a cause for encouragement. The Continental's belief in freedom, his willingness to die for that noble-seeming cause, the discharge of a weapon in his own life-loving hands. All of this traded for the cruel task of waiting, waiting not for Von Steuben to mold them into great warriors, but for King George to understand the futility in his attempt to maintain colonization of a land far larger than his own and separated by an ocean. It seems, in these conditions, that a rational Continental would be more likely to die of disillusionment than hunger.

Confession time, bro. Back when we were waiting for your body to land at Dover, I freaked. Big time. Dropped the F-bomb on Mom and Dad, the other families in waiting, the soldiers whose mission it was to maintain order amid a moment of lucidness that most will never experience. Cowards I called them, the ones who used a tripwire and an improvised explosive device to take you away from us. The lawyer and dad are building a defense around that moment, some mumbo-jumbo about the physiology of trauma, of symptoms untreated. But unlike Mad Anthony, bro, I do not extol my innocence, my victimization. I am guilty, we all are guilty, of escalating hatred. Marc Norris pushed my elbow only because I placed it where I had. Mine, alone, was the grip on the bayonet. I was the saber-rattling soldier a-howl at Beggerstown. We label the incident at Paoli a massacre, an act of savagery; yet, we applaud the earliest Revolutionary soldiers for 'waiting 'til they saw the whites of their enemy's eyes,' code for 'sneak attack' to those on the receiving end. Push a man at the height of his helplessness, then question the appropriateness of his response? No longer for me. A tripwire is what a man uses when he cannot stand up and fight fairly; a suicide bomber blood relative of the infamous British General Grey. Dad and his lawyer can convince themselves of whatever they like, but I know the depths of my own guilt.

Here is an inventory of what I lost in my most recent transition:
    My innocence
    My freedom
    My future
    The '98 Volvo and authentic Revolutionary War uniform
    The hope that Mom just might start smiling again

Here is an inventory of what I gained:

A bed in a Pennsylvania juvenile penitentiary

Countless hours of being left alone to consider the true nature of war

Insight into the sorry nature of mankind

I am sorry, Chas, about Afghanistan. The not writing and all. I didn't understand. There is so much, bro, I failed to understand.

-Dunc

WAYNE ANTHONY CONAWAY

Formerly Fearsome

It may be hard to believe today, but in my youth I was scary. Yes, I was once a tall, formidable-looking male who haunted the streets at night.

Years ago, upon my release from the military, I moved back to West Chester to attend college. I lived with my parents at the far north end of town, and attended West Chester University at the far south end. The distance between the two was almost a mile and a half. Lacking a car, I walked back and forth to classes, dressed in an increasingly-shabby military coat. I especially enjoyed walking at night, with the heels of my boots clacking on the concrete of the almost-deserted sidewalks. But I discovered that my very presence, looming out of the dark, could frighten other pedestrians. I wasn't the biggest guy in my town of 20,000 souls, but apparently I was one of the scariest.

Not having any desire to terrify strangers, I adjusted my behavior. When my path ahead would intersect with that of another pedestrian, I would change my pace—slowing down, or speeding up, or even crossing the street.

I also found more creative ways to appear less scary. For example, I found that I didn't frighten anyone if I kept my books visible. I always had a textbook or a novel with me, but the pockets of my military greatcoat were commodious enough to hold them in. Once I took a book out, I was no longer scary. (Apparently, no one has ever been mugged by a bookworm.)

As my finances improved, I discovered other techniques. I made an attempt to take up smoking. In and of itself this didn't make me less scary, but the process of lighting a cigarette provided an excuse to stop while other pedestrians moved on. (In true macho style, I tried lighting a friction match on my thumbnail, but I kept burning my thumb. Scary guys shouldn't say "Owie-ow-ow!") Later, I bought a cigarette case from a second-hand shop. While it wasn't visible from a distance, anyone who spotted such an effete accessory couldn't possibly be frightened of me.

I didn't go so far as to wear a necktie, which I've never been comfortable in. When I wanted to dress up, instead of a tie, I actually wore an ascot. No one is affrighted by a man wearing an ascot. They may wonder about his sexual preference, but they're not frightened.

I also tried wearing a top hat, but it kept blowing off in the wind. If I'd found a monocle, I'm sure I would've tried to wear that, too. Of course, the last individual who managed to carry off the top hat-and-monocle look was Mr. Peanut. He's not the kind of role model I prefer, since I have it on good authority that Mr. Peanut never got laid. (I don't know if it was the monocle or the fact that he lacked genitalia.)

Eventually, I bought a car. Being ensconced in a vehicle kept me from scaring pedestrians. To be more precise, it kept me from frightening them with my appearance...I could still frighten them with my driving. (I'm sure it will only take me another 20 years to learn how to parallel park.)

And the car made me unscary in another way. It allowed me to stop walking three to six miles a day However, I continued to eat as if I was still a peripatetic pedestrian. If you want to lose your fearsomeness, there's no better way than gaining twenty pounds. (Which I did...five times in a row.)

Nowadays, as I wheeze from parking lot to restaurant, I don't scare anyone. Sometimes I miss that young, svelte, scary guy I used to be. But my hair is turning gray, so I'd be unscary now, even if I was thinner.

Of course, I don't smoke, carry a cigarette curse, or wear an ascot anymore, either. So it's not all bad.

WAYNE ANTHONY CONAWAY

Fit for a King

You've heard the ads warning that "80% of women are wearing the wrong bra size" and offering expert sizing. Well, now men can benefit from the same expertise.

Littlefield's Sports Emporium is now offering free sizing for men, to insure that they're wearing an athletic supporter that fits properly. "I don't have any statistics on how many men are wearing the wrong size supporter," says owner Irving Littlefield. "But it's a lot. We've ordered a wide range of sizes, and now we can fit anyone."

While I've never noticed that my jockstrap wasn't fitting properly, I was intrigued enough to pay Littlefield's a visit. A sign in the window boasted "Sports Garments Fit for a King...or Queen!" Mr. Littlefield himself directed me to a fitting room. "Strip from the waist down. You can keep your socks on."

"Shoes?" I asked.

"Not unless you wear those shoes while engaging in sports activity."

Since I was wearing pair of tasseled Bass Weejuns with Cuban heels, I took them off when I got inside the fitting room, along with my trousers and boxers. Unlike most fitting rooms in New York City, this one had a full-length door with a lock. I wondered how I was to be sized up.

I was only half-nude for a moment before I heard a curtain pulled back. What had appeared to be a full-length mirror on one wall was now transparent!

I felt like I was inside one of those peep show booths with a live nude woman on the other side, of the sort that used to be found in Times Square before it got gentrified.

However, the woman on the other side of the glass wasn't a stripper. She was an elderly Jewish lady, fully clothed. She looked like my ex's Aunt Shlomit, right down to her air of exasperated disappointment in me.

According to my female colleagues, this is exactly the sort of woman who usually worked in the bra-sizing business. In fact, I later found out that she specialized in sizing customers for sports bras at Littlefield's.

She pulled out a small notebook and a pencil. "Let's get started," she said. "Turn around, slowly."

I complied.

"Fine. Now I need you to spread your legs, as far apart as you can. Brace your hands on the walls, so's you don't fall down."

I struggled to obey. After standing in the horse position for over a minute while she scribbled on her pad, the strain started to get to me. After all, I hadn't limbered up first. "I'm getting a cramp!"

"Then be glad I don't make you do a split. OK, get up on the Step-E-Sizer, and we're done."

Next to me was an apparatus the size of an Ottoman. It was one of those motor-less step exercisers, for people who can't afford to join a gym and use a Stairmaster. I placed my feet on the pedals and got aboard.

"Step up and down. I need to see you move." She made another note. "You play the baskety-ball?"

"Uh, yes. And soccer."

"Soccer! My 8-year-old granddaughter plays soccer! What's wrong with baseball, huh? Big man like you, you afraid of getting spiked?"

She sighed, an ineffable Ashkenazi exhale that said she still hadn't forgiven the Dodgers for moving to Los Angeles.

"You always say what you think out loud, smart guy?" she snapped.

"Sorry. I'm a writer—"

"And it's the Giants I miss. Not everyone's from Brooklyn!" She put her notebook away in an apron pocket. "Enough, we're done. You need a 46 waist, cup size "A.""

"Uh, an A cup. Is that good?"

"What am I, your girlfriend? If your pizzle works right, be happy with it. Someday it won't." She stuck her pencil in her hair. "Get dressed. I'll have your size ready at the counter."

"How big is the selection of styles?"

"Victoria's Secret this ain't. You got a choice of white or black. But it'll fit."

And she vanished behind the curtain.

A week after purchasing my expertly-sized jockstrap from Littlefield's, I have to admit that she was right. Thanks to the proper equipment, I now have a vertical leap of over six inches when I play the baskety-ball. And I bounce a lot less now that I have an expertly-sized sports bra, too.

TERRY HEYMAN

The Ocean's Breath

Deborah wasn't interested in meeting anyone but her mother was insistent. She told Deborah that she needed "to get out there" and that the whole idea of "taking a break" was pure and utter nonsense. Her cancelled wedding was old news, and besides, her mother had already given Ted her phone number. Deborah forgot her mother's words as soon as she had heard them, as was her habit in recent months. She continued the routine of her daily life so it surprised her when, exactly ten days later, Ted called. Deborah had just settled into her usual position, nestled in the corner of her oversized velvet sofa. The universal remote was at her hip and a bowl of microwave popcorn rested on top of a damask pillow stationed in her lap. She let out a dramatic sigh and grabbed the cordless. The unfamiliar voice was deep and energetic. Ted explained how Deborah's mother and his mother had become recently acquainted. He made a lame joke about Deborah's mother flashing her photo like a matchmaker from the old country.

A tiny groan escaped her. She knew the photo. It was taken at her college graduation two years earlier. The camera caught her laughing, confident of her brilliant future. "You could model with this picture," her mother had said. Her long dark hair was tangled and twisted on itself, caught in an unexpected wind. Deborah's mother laminated the photo at a copy shop and carried it tucked inside a side pocket of her purse.

"So you're a lawyer," said Ted.

"I'm not a lawyer," Deborah corrected.

"That's what your mom told my mom."

"No, she says 'I go to court *like* a lawyer.' I'm a proba-tion officer." Deborah walked into her spotless kitchen. She poured a generous amount of warm white wine into a crys-tal goblet and tossed in two ice cubes from the freezer. She learned Ted was thirty-six years old and had never been married. This is what it had come down to. After the *disaster*, as in — *the canceled reservations, all those lost deposits, a real dis-aster that Richard turned out to be* — Deborah's mother felt compelled to get involved in her romantic life. "I'm your mother. Let me fix whatever needs fixing." It wasn't that Deborah didn't want to meet someone new; it was that she felt marked by the whole episode. The humiliation clung to her like stale perfume.

Ted did most of the talking while Deborah finished her wine. After twenty minutes he asked if she wanted to meet for a drink. Deborah agreed without hesitation. They didn't have much in common, but from the moment Ted uttered his first syllable to her, she knew she would say yes to a date if he asked, if for no other reason than to satisfy her mother.

At first, Deborah wondered what had happened with her and Richard. She'd revisit pivotal scenes in her mind, replaying them, changing the dialogue, altering the out-come. They met sophomore year at Boston University. Deborah was immediately struck by his maturity. At twenty years old, Richard told Deborah he wanted two children, a boy and a girl, in that order, and wore a tie on the weekends for the hell of it. She spent most of her free time in his off-campus apartment studying and learning new recipes in his kitchen. His was the nicest place she had ever seen a student live. Between Richard's high thread-count sheets and lush covering of chest hair, she felt warmed and sheltered by him. Deborah was in love for the first time in her life. Clear in his ambition to become a lawyer, Richard majored in po-litical science. Deborah was less focused. She thought about majoring in art history or architecture or painting, but after a mediocre grade in her studio class she settled on sociology instead. Sociology would enable her to graduate at the same time as Richard, which seemed like the important thing at the time.

Right before final exams senior year, Richard presented Deborah with a two carat diamond engagement ring. Deborah instantly said *yes*. Over the summer they moved into their new townhouse on the Main Line, not far from where Richard was to start law school at Penn. Deborah found a job in West Chester working at the courthouse in the probations department. While she didn't especially love the work, she came to appreciate it for giving her the ability to discuss criminal law with Richard and be home in time to take care of dinner. She reveled in the certainty of her life laid out neatly before her like a game of solitaire.

By mid-year, Deborah had become restless and lonely. She complained that she spent her days with drug addicts, collecting disgusting warm urine in plastic containers. She was ignored by her clients and their attorneys. She felt useless, like state-mandated window dressing. Richard was too pre-occupied with his studies to give her much attention. She got to know a few of her co-workers but making friends was hard. "Poor princess, big rock, small cock," she overheard another probation officer say loudly in the next cubicle. Deborah was sure he was talking about her.

When spring finally replaced the dank Philadelphia winter, it seemed Richard came home only to sleep and change his clothes. He said he preferred to study at the library and eating his meals on campus was simply more convenient.

One rare evening, Richard and Deborah were watching TV together while lying in their mahogany four poster bed.

"Do you think we're getting a little boring these days?" He adjusted the pillow beneath his head. "We act more like roommates."

"I'm not bored. I miss you though." She nudged toward him and started raking her fingers through his chest hair.

Richard looked up, his eyes locked on some imaginary point on the ceiling. Deborah stared at his fine profile in the silence. He stilled her hand and put the TV on mute.

"Maybe we should take a break."

"What are you talking about?" A pure uncomplicated fear rose inside of her. Their wedding date was set for New Year's Eve. Richard kept staring at the ceiling. The space between them was huge and glacial. The words, suspended in her throat, floating, waiting to be spoken. "Is there someone else?" It came out like a little girl's whisper.

Richard sighed. "No. Not really." Then he added, "Maybe. I don't know." He turned toward her and saw the panic move across Deborah's perfectly proportioned face. "It's not like that. She's just a friend from school. Nothing's happened."

"So what is it then?" Her face felt hot. She willed herself not to cry.

"I don't know really. It's just that I can't stop thinking about her and I want to be fair to you."

"Fair to me? This is being *fair* to me? We're engaged!" Deborah's voice broke on *engaged* and her eyes flooded with tears.

"I'm sorry. *Fair* probably wasn't the best word. But how can we be right for each other if I'm constantly thinking about someone else?"

"Constantly." The word echoed in her head, its full meaning sinking in. "You're constantly thinking about her, but nothing happened? Are you sure?" She was sobbing hard now.

"Yes I'm sure."

"I don't believe you — you're never around! Maybe you did sleep with her?" Deborah got up from their bed and started pacing the room.

"I didn't sleep with her." Richard sat up but stayed where he was.

"You didn't do *anything* with her?" She looked at him hard. "Tell me the truth. I deserve that much *at least*."

"Okay — one kiss."

"Jesus Fucking Christ! Are you in love with her?" Deborah went to the bathroom to grab a tissue. Her face was covered with red splotches and her nose looked like it belonged to an alcoholic.

"No, of course not," Richard said when she came back into the room.

"What's her name?"

"It doesn't matter, you don't know her."

"What does she look like?"

"What difference does it make?"

"It makes a difference to me!" Deborah yelled. "Is she prettier than me? Tell me!"

Richard breathed deeply. "No," he admitted. "She's not."

Deborah thought that would make her feel better, but in fact it made her feel worse. It wasn't beauty that stole Richard away, but something deeper, richer, harder to define, and harder to compete with.

"What am I suppose to do now?" The tears started up again.

"Look. I'm not saying it's over between us. All I'm saying is that I want some time to figure things out. I mean we've been together for so long and really, we're each other's first serious relationship. I'm asking you to be patient with me. I feel like I've been on this track my whole life, college, law school, marriage and I want a breather. I need to figure out what I really want."

"So are you going to quit school too?"

"No. I still want to be a lawyer," he said quietly.

"You just don't want to be married to me." She said it more to herself.

"Come here." He reached for her. "I love you. You know that, right." He was gentle with her now, perhaps feeling contrite. Deborah let herself be held. They lay together in their bed, the thin cotton jersey of her nightshirt separating his flesh from hers. She was certain she wanted to be with Richard. She knew she could be whatever he needed. A sudden urge overtook her. Deborah took hold of the hem of her nightshirt and lifted her arms. She raised the shirt over her head before Richard grabbed her wrists so roughly it shocked her. He forcibly brought her hands to her sides and smoothed the nightshirt back down over her bare chest.

He shook his head. "Don't."

"Why not?" Deborah cried.

"Isn't it better to know now if it's not right instead of making a decision that we could both regret for the rest of our lives?" His fingertips stroked the wetness off her cheeks. "The heart has its reasons which reason does not know."

"What does that even *fucking* mean?" Deborah cried harder.

Two weeks later Deborah moved out of their townhome and gave back the ring. Oh the *shandeh*! Her mother found her a one bedroom apartment on East Evans Street in West Chester, walking distance to the courthouse, and filled it with expensive furniture paid for with the money intended for her wedding. "After what you've been through, you deserve something better than Ikea." She lived alone in an exquisite honeymoon suite of her mother's making.

In those first months, her mother called daily. Deborah said she was okay, but of course, it was a lie. She was watching too much television, sometimes ten hours straight on Saturdays and Sundays. Microwave popcorn for dinner became standard. She obsessively checked Facebook and read the comments of college friends who were engaged, in grad school or were pregnant for God's sake!

"U look great!"

"Your baby bump is soooooooooooooo cute!"

"Being with my sorority sisters again SUCH a special day ☺. That's real friendship. Love you all . . ."

It awakened an unknown envy deep within her, so excruciating and raw; she couldn't have imagined its existence prior. She continued at her job in the probation department. The days slid one into the next with no distinction.

At times, Deborah became wistful. She remembered being nine years old. She'd crawl into her parent's darkened bedroom and slip into bed with her mother who often napped on Sunday afternoons after staying out late with her father on Saturday night. Her mother lay on her back, to avoid creating wrinkles while she slept, her hands resting on top of one another on her stomach. The heavy silk drapes were drawn shut, blocking the midday sun. Deborah thought it was the most wonderful and luxurious thing a person could do, to turn their back on the day's demands and selfishly take to one's bed. Deborah moved slowly, careful not to wake her mother as she adjusted the wool camp blanket over both their bodies. She allowed herself to become hypnotized by the steady rise and fall of her mother's chest. Inhale. Exhale. Inhale. Exhale. Her mother's soft snoring filled the room. It was like the crashing of the waves. She'd pretend she was at the beach in Ocean City where they rented a house on Asbury Street. Sometimes her mother would sense Deborah next to her and draw her close, spooning their bodies together. "Lie still," her mother would murmur. Deborah would wiggle her feet against the scratchy wool. The rough texture felt like sand slipping through her toes. Her mother's warm breath was the ocean breeze, tickling the back of Deborah's neck.

Deborah walked into the packed bar during happy hour. She noticed the men, dressed in suits, who looked as if they had come straight from work. Small groups of women surrounded them like satellites, all wearing a variation of the same uniform: high heels, jeans and a low-cut top that showed off tanned, speckled cleavage. Deborah wore an ivory silk blouse hung loosely over slim jeans. Her heels put her already substantial height just shy of six feet. A draft caught her blouse as she entered and she moved across the polished wood floor like a classic day sailor. A man sitting alone at the corner of the bar caught her eye, nodded, and walked toward her. Tall and meaty, his head was covered in dark coarse hair and he had deep set brown eyes. He was not a particularly handsome man. He wore a dress shirt, slacks, and cologne, which Deborah smelled at five feet away. She didn't hold out much hope for the evening and made a mental note to leave after one drink.

"I'm Ted." He offered his hand.

Deborah shook it and they found two empty seats at the bar.

"Does your Mother fix you up a lot?" he asked her.

"I could ask you the same thing."

"No. I can find my own dates, thank you very much." He chuckled, as if recalling a private joke. "But she said if I called you, I wouldn't be sorry." Deborah smiled weakly at the compliment.

They sipped their drinks and Ted told her about his business. He was in retail and sold sewing machines, fabrics, buttons, patterns, that kind of thing. He personally gave lessons with the sale of each machine. Deborah was content to let him do most of the talking. Ted liked to talk. He said that when Hispanic ladies came into the store, he'd have to explain everything to them in Spanish. He added that he wasn't truly bilingual, but knew enough to get through the Viking sewing manual and the Cancun airport. His eyes shone as he spoke passionately to Deborah, laying out his plans for expanding his business, opening more stores, appealing to different demographics.

She smiled. She liked this eagerness to impress. She studied him closely and ordered a second Cosmopolitan. Ted was full of stories of Mexican vacations and parties at well-known restaurants in town. She changed her mind about him. His face had the look of a younger man, a man unencumbered by a wife and kids. She surprised herself by laughing at his increasingly tasteless jokes.

Ted whispered in her ear, "How do you circumcise a redneck?"

"How?"

"Kick his sister in the chin." He laughed and took a gulp from his gin and tonic.

Deborah touched her ear where Ted's breath had been. She was getting buzzed. She found Ted's lack of refinement appealing, honest and earthy. She could tell he liked her.

When he walked Deborah to her car, he took her hands in his. "I think you're a very special person," he said before putting his lips to her cheek. She could still smell his lingering cologne.

They soon fell into a pattern of speaking regularly. Deborah told Ted about her job as a probation officer. Deborah believed she was meant to do something else with her life, but had no idea what. Growing up, Deborah's mother filled her head with the notion that they were special. "Our family always did well. We are all educated and have good marriages. A family of doctors and lawyers you come from. Everyone is naturally thin and barely any cancer either. This is your gene pool too, Deborah. There's no shame in being more fortunate than other people." Lately Deborah feared she wasn't as fortunate as her mother liked to believe.

"How can you tell if you're wife is dead?" Ted asked.

"How?" It was late to be on the phone. They both had to get up early the next morning.

"The sex is the same, but the dishes pile up." Ted laughed.

Deborah laughed too, but not as much. She wasn't in the mood for his jokes tonight. She craved something else from him.

"Talk to me in Spanish," Deborah whispered into the receiver. She lay in bed, her bare legs sweeping from side to side underneath the loosely tangled sheets.

"La aguja de baja automaticamente."

"What did you say?"

"The needle lowers automatically."

"Seriously."

"Ok, seriously," Ted said. "Estas promino fin de semana libre?"

"What does that mean?"

"Are you free next weekend?"

"Si."

Deborah felt rejuvenated by the crass way Ted interrupted her pedestrian life. She started fantasizing about their potential future. She imagined helping Ted run his business, forgetting that she knew nothing about sewing machines or retail. *Ted & Deb.* She liked the feel of her tongue striking the roof of her mouth when she said their names together, *Ted & Deb.* Like a favorite song stuck in her head, she kept repeating it. *Ted & Deb* as she put on her makeup, *Ted & Deb* as she dried her hair. *Oh we have to invite Ted & Deb. He's so funny but you know it's really Deb who's the brains behind the business.* She was more upbeat than she had been in months. People began to notice.

"You seem very smiley these days," said her friend Rachel. Rachel worked in probations with Deborah. She was older and married to a successful defense attorney in town. Rumor around the office was she had been trying for years to get pregnant. Rachel took an instant liking to Deborah claiming she always wanted a little sister.

"Uh-huh" said Deborah. They were eating lunch at their favorite salad spot on Gay Street.

"Uh-huh. What's that? Did you inherit some money? Meet someone?"

"No." Deborah didn't want to share yet. She wasn't sure what her friend would think of her sewing machine salesman.

"So what then?" Rachel demanded.

"Nothing. Can't a person just be happy?" Deborah sighed. She finished her drink and threw her leftovers into the garbage.

"No, a person can't." Rachel pulled out a compact and did a quick check for food in her teeth. "Not without a reason, they can't." She carefully re-applied her lipstick then gave Deborah a suspect look. She knew a lie when she heard one. She should have been a lawyer.

On Saturday, Deborah got up early for a manicure and pedicure. She chose sheer pink for her fingers and dark purple for her toes. Next, she went to the hair salon for a blowout. When the stylist asked Deborah if she had any special plans for the evening, Deborah answered "I'm meeting my fiancé for dinner . . . in town." "Nice," the stylist answered. Deborah felt a rush of guilt. She knew she was being idiotic, but she missed being able to say *my fiancé*. Later, she carefully shaved her legs, underarms and bikini area and slipped into a new dress shortly before Ted arrived to pick her up. They drove to Skool in Ted's BMW. The club was located in what used to be a private prep school. There was a small crowd of people at the entrance when they arrived. Ted walked up to the bouncer and less than a minute later, they were ushered inside. It took her eyes a few minutes to adjust to the darkness. Ted grabbed her hand and led her through the dense crowd as Michael Jackson shrieked "wanna be startin' something." They climbed a glass staircase to the second floor where Ted greeted another bouncer guarding the entrance to a private room. Again, they were allowed to enter. Small groups of people clustered together on leather banquettes, their faces eerily lit by lighted cocktail tables dotting the room. *The Teacher's Lounge* written in giant neon script hung in midair, suspended from the ceiling. Deborah settled into a seat at the edge of the balcony affording her a view of the entire club. She gazed out over the sea of beautiful, aching bodies moving below. "In this life, you're on your own. And if the elevator tries to bring you down, go craaaaaaazy," Prince sang. Ted started talking. Deborah couldn't follow his jokes over the loud music. She had to ask Ted to repeat himself so many times that she just gave up. She was on her second Cosmopolitan when Steve, the club manager came over to greet them.

"Steve, I've got one for you," said Ted. "What do you call a woman paralyzed from the waist down?" He paused for effect. "Married."

"Speaking of married, Ted, is your wife here tonight? I want to introduce her to Deborah." Steve's voice had an abrasive quality that made Deborah instantly dislike him.

"No, she wasn't feeling well so I left her home." Ted let out a howling laugh. He looked at Deborah and she arched an eyebrow. "I'm joking," he said and placed his hand on her knee. He turned to talk to Steve again, letting his fingers linger on her skin, tapping her bare thigh in time to the music.

Time moved silky smooth. Prince became Madonna who became Duran Duran who became Soft Cell who became Falco—eighties night at Skool. Midway into her third Cosmopolitan, Deborah felt herself grow slick, as if any moment she might slide off the sofa and melt into an oily puddle on the floor. She asked Ted to take her outside for air. As they made their way, Deborah tripped—more a function of the alcohol than her platform heels. Ted caught her and she continued to lean into him as they moved forward. The parking lot smelled of cigarettes and garbage. "My apartment is not too far from here," Ted noted.

The small one-bedroom was filled with standard man stuff: a black leather sofa, matching leather chair and a chrome and glass coffee table. In the bedroom was a wood sleigh bed made up with Ralph Lauren linens. She assumed his mother decorated the bedroom.

"I thought you might want this." Ted held out a glass of water.

She looked into his questioning eyes and saw the possibilities in front of her. She could ask him to take her home now or stay the night. She brushed Ted's hand as she took the glass from him and leaned into his chest. Ted's sausage lips instantly covered hers. He was a gentle kisser which surprised Deborah. They had sex and Ted turned chatty. "You're so gorgeous" he said. "You feel amazing" he said. Afterwards Deborah noticed that the hair on his head wasn't mussed at all, like a helmet it laid there. He curled his body around hers and started humming *Der Kommissar* tapping out the bass line on her thigh. Neither spoke. Deborah could make out the outline of his furniture but just barely. Buzzed and dehydrated, she surrendered herself to the unfamiliar darkness. She pulled the covers high and offered Ted her back, on which he immediately started writing script letters with his finger tips.

"No offense because I mean this as a compliment. You have a really nice body, but at first I wasn't sure because that dress you wore tonight makes you look a little heavy," said Ted.

"You must be used to girls who wear tight clothes and know nothing about fashion," Deborah murmured before nodding off.

Deborah's mother was yelling. She always yelled when she talked on her cell phone. "What's he like? Is he nice?"

"Yes, he's nice. Funny. He makes me laugh." Deborah said and poured herself a glass of wine.

"A man who can make you laugh is important."

"We went back to his apartment after the club." She took a healthy sip then added, "It was just okay." She threw in that last part like a dare. Would her mother think she was referring to the apartment or to the sex? Deborah hadn't always been so churlish with her mother, but her broken engagement had given her a kind of freedom, a pass on polite conversation. Sometimes when she was in a mood, Deborah blamed her mother for what happened with Richard. Oh, not really. But Deborah took it out on her. Why didn't she at least warn Deborah this could happen, that she could be tossed aside by the man she loved as casually as a shirt needing to go to the dry cleaners? How could her mother, married to the same man since age nineteen, possibly advise her on *anything?* Deborah heard her mother exhale her cigarette smoke. Deborah drained her glass.

"Is that what's important to you now?" Her mother sighed.

Deborah didn't know what was important anymore.

Rachel had seen the large flower box waiting for Deborah on the receptionist's desk. That was typical Rachel, looking at everyone else's mail when she picked up her own. She asked Deborah what Ted did for a living with a mouth so stuffed Deborah could see she ordered the Cobb this time.

"He owns a button store." Rachel repeated Deborah's words like she was learning a foreign language.

"It's not just buttons, its fabrics and sewing machines too. He let me pick out anything I wanted and I chose these beautiful enamel ones. I'm going to put them on that jacket I have, the one that looks like a Chanel," Deborah said.

"It doesn't look like a Chanel."

"Yeah it does." Reflexively, Deborah looked down at the jacket she was wearing and wondered what Rachel thought of it.

"Sorry, not even close. I just don't think you should be walking around thinking it looks like one thing, when it looks like another," Rachel said between gulps of diet iced tea.

"Ted's also fluent in Spanish." Deborah changed the subject.

"*Muy bien!* So is this serious? Are you in love?"

"No, but I *might* fall in love with him." Deborah was irritated now. Who was Rachel to judge her boyfriend? She could quite possibly fall in love with Ted, open up a chain of retail stores, *Ted and Deb*. He was into her, that much was sure. He peppered his conversations with *hey sexy*, and *sleep well, gorgeous*. So what if it was a little blatant, she liked it.

"Just make sure you're not settling because of what happened with Richard." Rachel's voice went low, "lots of other attorneys out there, you know." Deborah felt herself stiffen. She forgot how critical Rachel could be at times.

Ted stood in Deborah's bedroom admiring a painting on the wall. It showed a girl peering at her reflection in a mirror, her face hidden from the viewer. It was part of Deborah's junior year studio collection. It was judged to be a tired cliché of artist exploring identity and all that typical art school crap. At the time, Deborah was crushed by the harsh critique but she still liked the painting enough to hang it in her bedroom. Ted wanted to see more. He thought dating an artist was sexy. He slowly flipped through her portfolio, lingering on some pages longer than others. He was no expert by any means, but to his unsophisticated eye, Deborah had honest-to-god talent. He studied an abstract nude for a few moments, trying to determine if it was a self-portrait. He asked if he could have the painting so that Deborah could always be naked in his apartment. Annoyed, Deborah packed up her portfolio and slid it back under her bed.

"Don't be so sensitive, I was making a joke," he said.

"I know it was a joke and I'm not sensitive."

"Yeah, you are." He said it not unkindly, but matter-of-fact, as if he was describing the weather. "*You* are a sensitive artist. I like that." He growled and nuzzled her neck.

"Is everything about sex with you?" She pushed him off her.

"No. Not everything." Ted grabbed her hand and pulled her next to him on the bed. "Ok, you want Mr. Sensitive? I can be Mr. Sensitive. I like your paintings."

"Thank you."

"Are you painting anything now?"

"No."

"Why?"

"Why?" Deborah repeated. *Why* rolling around in her head, an entire collection of *Whys*, noisy, aimless, like tin cans in the gutter on a windy day. Why? Why? Why? Why am I not painting? Why am I not married to Richard? Why am I working for probations? Why anything? Deborah sighed. "I'm just not painting now." She didn't feel like taking anymore and walked into the bathroom. It was getting late and they needed to shower and change. They were going to a party at Rachel's house. Half the office would be there and Deborah had gamely decided to bring Ted. Deborah showered first and was putting on her make-up when Ted kicked open the bathroom door.

"*Jesus Fucking Christ, Deborah!*" he screamed. "I just burned myself in your shower." Deborah looked in amazement at Ted who stood wet and naked. Water ran off him, soaking the white carpet. She hadn't really *seen* him, not fully, not in daylight. His brash nakedness next to her antique vanity, crystal lamp, and bed dressed in pristine white linens jolted her.

"Jesus Deborah, your *fucking* shower! I just *fucking* burned myself in your *fucking* shower where the water is so *fucking* hot you can make *fucking* spaghetti! He stood in a gray puddle of Berber. "I can't believe it. I turned the faucets toward each other like I always do and it caused the hot to go all the way up and the cold all the way off. What kind of *fucking shower* does that?"

Why was this her fault? *"What-kind-of-person-does-that-in-a-strange-shower-without-knowing-how-the-faucets-work?"* She emphasized each word as if speaking to one of her drug-addicted clients.

"Deborah, I'm really hurt here!"

"Okay, I'm sorry." She grabbed a towel and handed it to him. "Come. Sit down."

Ted slouched down on the bed soaking the white comforter and Deborah gave him another towel. His chest and shoulders were bright red beneath black matted hair. He looked like giant road kill. "You're a teensy bit red but I think it will be fine," Deborah offered.

"Maybe I need to go somewhere?"

"Go where?"

"You know the ER, have someone take a look at this?"

"Are you kidding? You don't need to go to the ER for this."

"But it hurts." Ted actually pouted when he said the words.

She stared at him, his tummy pooched over the towel. Repulsion and empathy began sparring inside of her. "We'd just be wasting our time. We'd sit there for hours, miss the party and they won't do anything anyway," Deborah said as nicely as she could manage.

Ted got up to examine himself in her mirror. "But, it really hurts."

"Hold on. Maybe I have something." Deborah started pulling out the multitude of shampoos, hair sprays, nail polish, makeup, blow dryers, flat irons and hair brushes from underneath her bathroom sink, but found no sunburn cream.

They stopped to buy Solarcaine spray on their way to the party. Ted slipped the can into his coat pocket as they pulled up in front of the enormous house with its fake brick facade. Though Rachel and her husband Josh bought the house two years ago the landscaping was still nonexistent. Admittedly, Rachel was a great hostess even if she obsessed over food. She was always telling Deborah "you can never be too rich or too thin." She was well on her way to both Deborah noticed.

"Everything I serve is very healthy, low or nonfat, even the chicken salad is nonfat," Rachel said pointing out the buffet. The table was exquisite. Colorful serving dishes with watermelon and feta salad, thinly sliced marinated flank steak, chicken salad, whole grain artisan bread, skewers with grilled shrimp and pineapple, low fat crème fraiche for dessert.

"It all looks amazing" said Deborah.

"There's no such thing as nonfat chicken salad," said Ted.

"Yes there is. I made it with nonfat mayo," answered Rachel.

"Nonfat mayo doesn't exist." Ted turned and winked at Deborah. She looked back at him as if he were drowning kittens.

"It doesn't exist? Of course it exists. I bought it!" Rachel said, her voice rising.

"I've never seen nonfat mayo, low fat, yes, but not nonfat. Maybe you made a mistake." Ted smiled.

Seconds later, Rachel returned from the kitchen with a jar of fat-free mayonnaise and shoved it into his hand.

"Wow!" Ted whistled loudly. "I can't believe it. I've never seen this before. It must have just hit the stores today."

"Ted's just being funny," Deborah said with a feigned smile and slapped the air with her hand. She quickly excused herself to find the bar.

The house was full of people. Deborah hid out in the kitchen admiring the six burner stove and made small talk with her co-workers about the recent renovations Rachel had done. Periodically she peeked out to see what Ted was doing. He looked perfectly at ease in Rachel's living room. She joined him as he was discussing the difference in taste between nonfat and low-fat mayonnaise with the office receptionist. The nineteen year old receptionist appeared flattered by his attention. "Had anyone ever taken a shower so hot that they *literally* burned themselves?" he asked Rachel and Josh who joined them. Deborah tried to steer the conversation to a different topic, but Ted was encouraged by his audience. He unbuttoned the top three buttons of his shirt to expose his chest. Josh made a big show of examining Ted's shoulders to see whether any blisters had formed. Rachel tried to engage Deborah in a conversation about the crème fraiche promising it was "better than sex." The whole scene struck Deborah as doleful and she went to get another drink. From the kitchen window she could see their new swimming pool. She walked out the sliding doors into the backyard for a closer look. She recalled Rachel telling her it cost a fortune but it was worth the money for rock formations and a waterfall instead of a concrete hole in the ground. Dead bugs floated on the surface. It would be a few more weeks before the pool would be open for summer. Deborah kneeled and dipped her fingers into the cool water. She stayed for a moment making ripples with her hand. She wondered how it would go over if she left the party without telling anyone. How much time would pass before anyone noticed? Would people think she wandered drunk into the pool and drowned? Would Ted, in a dramatic attempt to rescue her, jump in only to learn that she had left without him? She laughed at the thought.

By eleven o'clock, they were back at Deborah's apartment. Ted plopped down on her sofa and turned on the TV.

"You know my back really does feel better. The Solarcaine was a good idea, Deborah. That was smart of you." He clicked through the channels. "It's getting late. Why don't I just stay here tonight?"

Deborah stared at the back of his head. She saw it now. This was how their life would be together. Sometimes she would laugh at Ted's jokes and sometimes she'd be embarrassed and resort to pretending to be tired or sick so she could go home early — it would be a lifetime of leaving the party early. She had tried with Ted. She really tried to keep an open mind about him but now saw it was hopeless. She would never fall in love with him.

"Do you have anything to drink?" Ted asked, his eyes still on the TV.

Deborah continued to stare at the back of his head. "I don't think we should see each other anymore," she said finally.

Ted turned and looked at her. "What's wrong?"

"I can't do this."

"I don't understand. What's wrong with you tonight?"

Ted kept talking but Deborah was no longer paying attention. It was all wrong, Ted, her job, her life, everything. Had it always been this way she wondered? What was her mistake? What had she *not* done? Was there some class she forgot to take in college that would have explained it?

"Talk to me," Ted said reaching for her. Without warning, Deborah's bones felt too heavy for her body. They were weighed down by sadness, confusion, rage, all mixed together, her own unique marrow, a sewage sludge coating the hollow interiors of her skeleton. Her face became hot and she could feel the tears. She needed to sit. Ted's confused face kept talking. "What did I do?" he said. But how could Deborah explain the utter wrongness of her life? It had been a slow growing cancer, silently invading her organs and tissues for years, this wrongness.

"Talk to me Deborah! Why won't you tell me what's wrong? I can help fix it." Ted was standing now, moving closer to her, pleading.

She laughed. Insane laughing, crazy laughing, because it was almost exactly what she had said to Richard on the night she moved out of their townhome. The tears moved freely now, marking her face in a haphazard pattern of black lines from destroyed mascara. Deborah didn't feel hysterical but knew she must have looked it, looked like a crazy person, like one of her own clients. And in her most resolved *talking-to-a-drug-addict* voice she said "I think you should go now, Ted." Exasperated, angry, he gathered his coat and Solarcaine.

"I'm sorry," she whispered as he walked past her and out of the apartment.

Once alone, Deborah calmly got into bed without bothering to change her clothes. She carefully arranged the pillows and pulled the white comforter over herself. She closed her eyes and lay still. She waited to feel the ocean's breath on the back of her neck. Quietly. Patiently. She prayed for it to come.

MICHAEL DOLAN

The River Runs Red

The man pushed in where most others put out.

A dam lay 200 yards downstream, and though the slow-moving water didn't seem to pose much of a threat, once you rounded the bend and realized what lie ahead it was usually too late.

The man didn't seem to care. He sat straight and stiff in his red canoe, arms moving slowly, evenly, purposefully. Each stroke of the paddle began and ended in near silence, and if the trails and river were quiet enough, you might be able to hear the pushing of water each time the paddle came up for a breath.

The giddy and gleaming couple paddling up to the riverbank certainly didn't notice the man as he passed by a few yards away. He tipped his hat toward the couple, smiling. Neither of them saw the gesture. The black cowboy hat perched atop his head. The black tee shirt tucked into matching jeans. His appearance called for attention and anonymity at the same time.

Drifting toward the riverbank, the girl had her left hand raised in the air, letting the newly placed engagement diamond shimmer in the sun. Todd snapped a photo.

A crowd on the riverbank hooted, hollered, and screamed in delight while a group of young children held up a sign that read: "Congratulations, Jenni and Todd!" Jenni squealed in surprise at seeing her family, joined by Todd's, standing by the water's edge. A tear rolled down her cheek as she looked over at Todd across the canoe.

"Thank you," she mouthed.

Todd simply smiled, a rush of relief and joy running through his veins. Proposing on a canoe was risky business, but given the amount of time he and Jenni had spent together on, in, and by the river, it only made sense. The ring hadn't fallen into the muddy water, she'd said yes, and their families had made it to the rendezvous point in time. It all went as orchestrated. Life was good.

Nearing shallow water, Jenni was out of the canoe and splashing toward the crowd before the canoe even touched bottom.

No one noticed the man in black as he paddled upstream and out of view.

Sammy climbed aboard and rushed to make sure he got a window seat. It was his first time on the train and he was going to take full advantage of it. He sat down on the edge of the vinyl bench and immediately bounced to his feet again in excitement. His hands reached toward the window and with all his strength he managed to force the latches sideways and pull the window open. Given the age of the coach, which was built in the 1930s, it was doubtful the window would even open. When it did, Sammy found himself both delighted and nervous that it opened as far as it did. A boy his age, even one not just six but going on seven, could easily tumble out that window if he wasn't careful. He quickly sat back on the bench. At that moment the train's whistle sounded through the air, wakening the old burgundy coach from its slumber, and the town along with it. The boy smiled and looked up at the man sitting beside him.

"Thanks for taking me on the train, Dad."

"Sure thing, Sammy."

The train pushed off and down the tracks they went. Eyes fixed out the window, Sammy discovered the town through an entirely new perspective. Here were the streets, buildings, and stores that he passed each day on the way to and from school, and yet they were somehow unfamiliar. Storefront awnings, road signs, and potholes in the streets—

all those landmarks the boy religiously kept inventory of during the back-and-forth drives to school—were all gone. In their stead were dumpsters, loading docks, central air units, dump trucks, and the littered and unkempt grounds of the town's backside.

"There's work," his father said, pointing out the window at the large steel factory just across an abandoned lot.

Sammy struggled to recognize the building. He had certainly been there enough to recognize his father's nine to five home-away-from-home. It was the same building he would visit after a trip to the doctors or on the way home after a half-day from school, carrying with him a surprise milk shake or Icee for his dad. But without the bump in the road, without the large block lettering on the front of the building, without the security guard at the parking lot entrance, the building remained a stranger. By the time Sammy was able to figure out where they were, the train was already bearing down on new, uncharted territory.

Soon the town gave way to trees and thickets as the train made its unhurried course south. The sound of snapping and snagging branches scraping against the side of the train kept Sammy's face from leaning too close to the open window. Wilderness was taking its stand here, fighting back against the vessel in its midst.

Once in the woods, the tracks followed the path of the winding river as both train and water traveled downstream. Sammy gazed at the water and the wild, imagining himself a great explorer discovering new lands.

"Hey, look at that, Dad!"

Sammy's father looked up from his phone in time to see water splash up from the surface of the river. A rope dangled from a tree branch reaching out over the water, dancing back and forth above the water's surface.

A head emerged from the water like a submarine's periscope, and Sammy watched as the boy swam toward the rope, grabbed a hold of it, and with a flick of the wrist sent it sailing toward the riverbank. Waiting hands standing on a giant rock at the water's edge reached out for their turn.

"That'll be you in another ten years, son."

"Really?"

His father smiled.

But ten years was an eternity to a boy of six. Such a discovery called for immediate action. It was like opening a remote control car on Christmas morning only to discover that Santa had neglected to deliver the required batteries.

"Can we go tomorrow, Dad?"

Sammy's father laughed. "How about a compromise? Let's call it five years."

"Okay," said Sammy, turning to look back to the river. The rope swing was long gone.

Staring out the window at the river, Sammy let his mind wander. He pictured himself on that rope swing – diving, jumping, and flipping into the cool water. Here was heaven, just a few miles from home, and it had been hidden from him all these years. Yes, all six of them. He dreamed of skipping ahead five years and waking up the next morning as a taller version of himself.

"Going on twelve," he whispered, and smiled at the thought.

Further down river, a man in a red canoe caught Sammy's attention. At this distance it was hard to see him clearly, but something about the man made Sammy shiver.

Slowly, evenly, purposefully, the man pulled himself upstream. Sammy stared at the man as he came around a bend in the river, drawing close enough to make out his black hat and shirt. Like an owl turning its head, the man in black looked up toward the train and caught the boy in his gaze. Sammy wanted to turn away but found that he couldn't. The man had caught him staring, and guilt filled the pit in Sammy's stomach.

The slow, even, purposeful paddling stopped as the man rested the oar across the sides of his canoe. He reached over the side and dipped his hand into the water, picking up what looked to be a yellow leaf floating along the surface. A small cloud of steam formed where his hand touched the water. Perhaps it's the haze, the boy thought. Then the man smiled at Sam, nodded his head toward him and tipped his hat. Sammy shuddered.

"Dad," Sammy nudged.

He looked up from his phone.

"What's up, Sam?"

"Did you see that guy?"

"What guy?"

They both looked out the window as the tracks began to veer away from the river and deeper into the woods.

"Nevermind."

Digby set up camp in his usual spot, an overlook along the bank accessible only through a long ago abandoned and overgrown trail. A giant elm tree dominated the overlook, leaving room only for an artist and his easel and providing shade enough for both, just as Digby liked it.

He'd found his little hidden paradise earlier in the spring purely by happenstance. He started off painting along the bank where the paddlers pulled out, but gradually moved upstream in search of solitude. Wherever he placed his easel, though, it seemed he couldn't quite escape the society in which he fancied himself only a periphery participant in anyway.

A hiker's dog would invariably run up to Digby and hound him with probing nose or manic jumping. Once, with the landscape before him almost fully replicated on the canvas, an overly curious Mastiff trotted right up to Digby, and with wagging tail, knocked over the easel. The canvas landed face-down on the grass.

"Sorry," the dog's owner called from a distance. "Get over here, Pugsy."

Then there were the overheard comments and uninvited conversations from passersby.

"Didn't he paint the same thing last week, Mom?"

"Nice painting there, boy. Keep it up and you'll be the next Bob Ross."

"Mind if I ask you what oils you're working with? Winsor and Newton? Gamblin? I prefer Sennelier myself."

"Excuse me, sir. Do you sell your paintings? I'm just curious. My niece sells her paintings at a gallery in Manhattan and I was just wondering if you knew her. She's about your age and went to Moore. Ever hear of Violet Ashe?"

All of which made Digby grateful for the day a snake slithered between his feet two months prior while he was mid-canvas.

The slight touch of something brushing by his ankle, and then over his toes, sent Digby's steady hand off course in the middle of a tree line. Looking down to discover a two-foot black snake at his feet, the one between his own legs nearly relieved itself. His sandals danced with a frantic hop, skip, and jump, and no sooner had Digby jumped atop the nearest rock did he discover that the visitor was a harmless water snake. Digby caught many a water snake just like this one when he was twelve. He wondered if he still had it in him. Laughing to himself, Digby gave chase.

He followed the snake as it darted through the grass, past thickets, and down an overgrown path leading toward the water. The snake slithered at full speed and Digby caught up to it in time to see it reach the elm tree and slide into the water. Digby stood on the overlook and watched as it glided across the surface of the water, moving slowly, evenly, purposefully.

Digby returned to that overlook each week, the elm and easel providing all the company he needed. A great blue heron seemed to think otherwise. Each week it joined Digby directly across the water in the shallows of the river's edge. For hours Digby stood at his easel while the heron waded and trolled the waters for food. The two became quick companions, one occasionally looking up from his canvas, the other occasionally looking up from the water. Both keeping watch.

The river separated the two, and neither considered crossing that line. An unspoken pact between two solitary creatures, brought together and yet held apart by the water before them. Today was no different, and as Digby neared finishing his painting, he looked back across the water to see if he left any details out.

The heron lifted her beak from the water, snapped at the small snake she had caught, and lifted her neck skyward. Down her gullet it went. Digby dipped his brush into the puddle of slate grey on his pallet and corrected the heron's blue plumage on the canvas.

Loud and furious croaking suddenly sounded from across the water. Digby looked up, only to see his friend in a state of distress. She paced back and forth in the shallows, splashing furiously with her wings. Then, without warning, she took flight, her wing-beats carrying her upriver just above the water's surface. In a state of unease, Digby failed to appreciate the bird's beauty as she sailed along the river, followed its path around the bend, and disappeared from view.

He hastily packed up his easel and canvas and tramped down the abandoned path, longing for the society he had suddenly begun to miss.

A moment later, a man in black came paddling upstream in a red canoe. Slowly, evenly, purposefully, he gave chase.

B.J. stood in the cool water, his feet sinking in the muddy riverbed while water flowed over his shoulders en route downstream. He reached toward the rope above him and latched onto it. With three flicks of his wrist, releasing the rope on the third, the rope sailed toward the elephant rock on the riverbank. Stacey caught hold of it on the first attempt.

"C'mon, Stacey," called B.J. from the water. "Let's see what you got!" Stacey gave a quick look back at Rebecca and Tommy, who sat drying off on a smaller rock beside her.

"How's the water?" she asked them.

"Not bad," answered Rebecca. "Cool, but not cold enough to show off your tits, Stace."

Stacey laughed, instinctively adjusted her bikini top, and then launched herself off the rock. The rope carried her out over the water, and when it reached its highest and furthest point, she let out a scream and flew into the air.

B.J. smiled as he watched Stacey sail through the air and splash into the water. She disappeared under the surface and let the coolness of the river flow through her pores. It was a coolness that seemed to seep into her soul, invigorating and energizing it, and she wished she could stay under the water much longer. Her legs kicked like a frog, an amphibious breaststroke that made her feel as if she belonged to the river.

His head turning like a periscope, B.J. waited for her to surface. Twenty long seconds passed and the smile on his face began to fade.

"Rebecca! Tommy! You see her?"

They stood up on their rocky perch and canvassed the water. B.J. quickly saw the look of worry on their faces, mirroring his own.

Despite kicking up mud and dirt, Stacey was still able to see through the hazy water as she gained her bearings and swam toward her target. She thrust toward the river floor, then pushed off the muddy surface with her feet and launched out of the water. Her arms and legs wrapped around B.J. from behind.

"Gotcha!" she whispered into his ear.

Rebecca and Tommy laughed and sat back down on the rock.

"You scared the hell of out me!"

Stacey laughed. B.J. began to laugh too. He turned around to face Stacey and their lips met, tongues touched, and in the privacy of the water, hands wandered. A rock splashed in the water a few feet away from them.

"How 'bout you two get an effing room?"

The couple broke lips and turned toward the riverbank. Tommy stood tall on the elephant rock, and tossed another rock in their direction.

"Hey! A little help with the rope!"

Stacey swam over to the rope and flung it toward Tommy. He pounded his chest and did his best Tarzan yell, then proceeded to cannonball into the water. He cast a splash halfway across the river.

While B.J. and Tommy took turns on the rope swing, Stacey joined Rebecca on the warm rock, where they shared a bag of chips and drank diet sodas.

"Did Abbey ever text you back?" asked Rebecca.

"Yeah. Said she was coming this morning. Had to work till noon, but was coming right from the shop."

Stacey thumbed away at her phone: *U still coming? Water is great today.*

A response came almost immediately: *I <3 U Stace.*

Staring at the screen, Stacey held the phone in her hand for a minute and waited for another text to arrive. It never came.

Stacey thumbed back: *?????*

"Don't know if she's coming or not," Stacey said, setting her phone down next to Rebecca and climbing up onto the elephant rock. She stood next to B.J., grabbed the rope out of his hands, and smiled. "My turn!"

Under the surface, Stacey's body again soaked in the coolness of the water. The world was quiet here and she kept swimming as deep and as far as her lungs would let her.

Without warning, the cool water turned icy cold and sent Stacey shivering to the surface. Her teeth chattered and she could see her breath with each exhale.

"You okay?" yelled B.J. from atop the rock.

"Yeah," Stacey replied, not believing her own voice.

As quickly as it had arrived, the cold patch passed, though faint traces of it lingered deep below the surface, taunting Stacey's treading legs. She made for the riverbank, swimming freestyle the entire way.

"What, no help with the rope?" asked Tommy, standing on the giant rock as Stacey reached the water's edge. She didn't hear his call for help. Lifting herself out of the water, she went straight for her phone.

"Is this a good one, Dad?"

Henry looked over at his son. Smiled. Nodded.

"Perfect, Pete. Remember – sidearm, and flick with your wrist."

The young boy positioned the smooth, flat rock in his hands as his father had taught him and gazed intently out at the water. This is the one, he told himself, and gave it a whirl.

Plop!

"Almost had it that time, Pete. You'll get the next one, I'm sure."

Pete wasn't sure he'd ever be able to skip a rock. It seemed the little accomplishments in life somehow eluded him. At almost ten-years-old, he still couldn't whistle, snap his fingers, blow a bubble, armpit fart, or skip a rock. He was determined to check one of these off his list today, and went off in search of more flat specimens on the riverbank.

Henry hurled a tennis ball into the river, calling for Penny to give chase. Before the ball even reached the water, the bloodhound bounded into the water and galloped toward it. When the river grew too deep, the gallop turned into a swim, and Penny's head skirted along the water like a beaver. She reached the bobbing ball, snatched it in her jaws, and swam back to shore.

Pete sent another rock sailing.

Plop!

"Keep trying, Pete. Almost got it."

While Pete tossed rocks, Henry tossed the worn and wet Penn 3. The ball had certainly seen better days. It was in Penny's mouth when they first met her at the Francisvale Home, and it was still there the day they picked her up from the shelter.

When they arrived home later that day and Pete opened the car door for her, Penny dropped the tennis ball at his feet. It seemed to be her way of telling him, "I'm home." Pete picked up the tennis ball and named the newest member of their family right then and there. He tossed the ball across the front yard, calling out: "Get it, Penny!"

That was nearly two years ago. Countless games of fetch later, with thousands of scents collected in its faded yellow fuzz, somehow that ball managed to survive. Whether an errant throw sent the ball deep into a patch of pachysandra or into the heart of forsythia shrubs, Penny always came out with it in her jaws. Once, a bad bounce sent the ball rolling into the street and down the gutter. Penny caught up to it just as it was about to disappear into a storm drain. "Lucky Penny" became her nickname that day.

Plop!

Another failed attempt. Henry saw his son's frustration, tossed the tennis ball as far upstream as he could to keep Penny busy, and went to give the boy another lesson in skipping rocks.

"Pete, the world record is fifty-one skips. Let's try to beat it!"

"I'd settle for just one, Dad."

"Okay, then. Here, let me see what rock you –."

At that moment, an unsettling howl split the air. It was Penny. She scampered back and forth on the bank, barking and baying, yawping and yelping.

"PENNY!" hollered Henry. She stopped for a moment to snarl and growl at the river, and then darted up and down the bank in a state of manic distress. The tennis ball bobbed its way downstream past Penny, but she stayed ashore. The hound howled to the heavens.

Henry scanned the river and spied a flotilla of orange inner tubes and green canoes coming into view upstream. They stretched the width of the river, floating down water. Penny continued her frenzied baying, and Henry quickly went to leash her. She grew more agitated as the tubers and paddlers approached, though to Henry she didn't seem to be barking at them.

Holding onto the leash with both hands, Henry watched the tubers draw closer. The canoers had bright green shirts, and as they got closer he could make out the writing on them: "Saint Malachi's River Run!"

The church group looked over at Penny as they passed. Some smiled, others waved. The tubers closest to the river-bank looked more than a bit nervous as they unsuccessfully tried to steer away from the shoreline.

Henry thought about hollering out to the group to put them at ease. Maybe an "I've got her" or an "It's okay – she's harmless." Given Penny's manic baying, both reassurances seemed rather pointless.

"SORRY," Henry shouted, though no one in the river could hear his apology above the barking.

He looked over at his son, still combing the bank for the perfect rock.

"C'mon, Pete. We've gotta get going now."

Henry turned and began to pull Penny back toward the trail leading to the parking lot.

"One last one, Dad," Pete said to himself, and picked up another rock. It was the length of his pointer finger and felt smooth in his grip. "Perfect," he said.

Pete took aim at the river and side-armed the stone a bit downstream from the pack of paddlers and tubers. The stone hit the water and skipped off of it. Not once. Or twice. But three times!

The boy began to smile in disbelief, but as the stone skipped off the water the third time, it came crashing into the side of a red canoe.

THUMP!

Pete's smile left his face and his stomach turned. He looked at the man in the red canoe and didn't know whether to run or face up to his wayward toss.

The man simply looked over at Pete and smiled. Then he turned his gaze forward and paddled up the middle of the river, moving slowly, evenly, purposefully. Canoes and tubes passed by on either side, heading downstream. The group did not seem to notice the man in black pass through them. Instead, they looked toward the boy on the riverbank.

"C'mon, Pete," Henry shouted from the trailhead. Penny was still baying. The boy ran.

"Eat another strawberry before you have any more chips."

Colleen pushed the basket of berries in front of the girls. Ella and Lizzy obliged.

"That goes for you too, Paul."

"Yeah, Dad!" The girls giggled.

Paul laughed and popped another chip. They sat next to each other at the picnic table, the twins sandwiched between Paul and Colleen as they munched away on peanut butter and jellies. The seating arrangement not only afforded each of them a clear view of the river, but it kept the sun at their backs as well.

"Girls, did Mom ever tell you about the day we met?"

"Paul," warned Colleen with a look.

"Yeah, Dad," groaned Ella. *Wayne's World*. You told us."

"No, that was our first date."

"And yet I still married your father."

"Don't listen to your mother, girls. That was a great movie."

"Romantic too." Colleen laughed.

"Anyway," continued Paul, "the day we met I was swimming right out there with your Uncle Billy." He pointed straight ahead. "We're tossing a tennis ball in the river and two pretty girls in a paddle boat come pedaling by. It was your Aunt Mary and your mom. Aunt Mary was dating your Uncle Billy at the time and she knew he was swimming with me that day."

"We did not know you were swimming that day, Paul."

Paul laughed and pretended not to hear Colleen.

"So the two of them snuck a paddle boat out from Whistling Bridge Park and paddled five miles down the river just so your mother could meet me."

"It was not five miles," Colleen stated, though she clearly remembered the pain in her knees and thighs that day.

"Five miles in a paddle boat, Mom?" Lizzy and Ella pried for the truth, giddy at this newfound knowledge.

"Okay, maybe," Colleen confessed. "But it was worth it. Your father was a keeper. "

"Yuck!" the twins screamed. Ella and Lizzy jumped up from the picnic table and ran down toward the river's edge.

"I wonder whatever happened to that paddle boat," said Colleen. Given the ridiculous task of paddling it five miles upriver that day to return it – and risk getting caught in the process – they simply moored it to a tree and there it remained all summer. By the following spring it was gone.

"MOM! DAD! LOOK!"

Paul and Colleen looked up just in time to see a great blue heron flying upriver. Each of its wings seemed longer than the twins themselves. The two girls stared in amazement at the beautiful creature. When it was gone, they turned around, mouths agape.

"Saw your first blue heron, girls," said Paul. "Pretty cool, isn't it?"

"Let's follow it, Liz," said Ella.

The two ran off, following the trail along the river's edge.

"Don't go too far ahead, girls," Colleen called after them. Paul and Colleen packed up their picnic wares and followed the twins down the path. They walked without hurry, giving their girls space enough to explore on their own. A little freedom would do them good. Just not too much.

"Hard to believe they'll be eight come Thanksgiving," said Paul.

"I know."

Colleen's response was distant, and her pace had slowed down. Paul looked back, and saw that she was tapping away on her phone.

"Please don't tell me you're checking-in at the river."

"And what if I am?"

"I may have to de-friend you." He reached to grab the phone from Colleen's hands.

"Hey! Look at this! Jenni just got engaged. Look!"

She held the phone up for Paul to see. There was Jenni, sitting in a canoe and holding an engagement ring out in front of her. Paul thought of the past seven years and wondered what life would have been like without Jenni. She had helped Colleen out with the twins when they were infants, and she was their go-to babysitter ever since. Many a day she was nothing short of a lifesaver. He felt his eyes watering up, an emotional mix of both pride and wonder at the passage of time.

"Todd didn't even have the courtesy to ask me for her hand in marriage," he joked.

"Just wait until it's Ella and Lizzy. I think they'll be carrying you down the aisle." Colleen wiped away a tear on Paul's cheek and gave him a kiss. "C'mon, let's go tell them!"

"ELLA! LIZZY! WAIT UP!"

The girls were too far ahead to hear their parent's call. They wandered down the trail as it snaked along the river, occasionally stopping to lift up a rock to see what critters might lie beneath. The trail veered closer to the water and opened up onto a wide embankment leading down to the water. Ella and Lizzy ran down the slope and stood with their feet at the water's edge, scanning the bank for anything interesting.

"Here's a good one," said Lizzy, squatting down and trying to lift a large rock embedded in the muddy ground. "It's stuck, El. Help."

Ella bent down next to her sister, and together they tried to pry the rock free. It didn't budge.

"One more time," said Lizzy. "One. Two. Three!" Lizzy pulled up but her fingers slipped on the wet rock and she fell backward into the water. "Hey, you didn't help!"

Ella didn't look at her sister. Her eyes were on the water. "Did you hear that?"

"What?"

"A phone ringing. I thought I heard a phone ringing."

They listened. All was silent for a moment, but then they heard a ripple in the water. Looking to their right, they saw a man in black pushing off the bank twenty yards upstream. He climbed into his red canoe and began to paddle downriver. He paid no notice to the girls as he passed, sitting straight and stiff and paddling slowly, evenly, purposefully.

"What's she doing?" Ella asked. She pointed to a spot above the water where the man had just pushed off. Lizzy spotted the girl too and shrugged her shoulders.

"I don't know."

A phone started ringing again on the river.

"It's hers."

"Yeah. How come she's not answering it?"

The two girls just stared.

"Hey," Ella called out. "Your phone's ringing."

The girl didn't answer.

"Hey, girls," called Colleen when she spotted the twins and started down the slope toward the riverbank. "Guess what!"

Ella and Lizzy didn't turn around. The phone had gone silent and their eyes were transfixed upstream.

"Girls! Guess who's getting married!"

"What the – ?" Paul took off running through the water.

Colleen followed her daughters' eyes. Her shriek echoed down the river for miles, a primal scream filling all who heard it with instant and utter dread. She pulled Lizzy and Ella tightly against her, covering their eyes with her hands. There was no one there to cover her own eyes.

The tree reaching out over the river. The rope slowly swaying. The girl's reflection in the water.

In the silence of the river, a phone began to ring.

ELI SILBERMAN

The Great Neck Nazi Killer

Rebecca Epstein Cohen had carried the first bag of groceries into the kitchen of her four bedroom brick house on
Wensley Drive in Great Neck, Long Island and the phone
rang just as a long dormant memory surfaced, perhaps trig-
gering it, of the Nazi officer shoving her father, kicking him
to the ground and firing two shots into his head. Putting the
full Shop Rite bag on the counter she reached to the wall
phone hearing her younger sister's screams and mother's
sobs. It had been years since the last flashback and she was
shaken by the clarity, the vividness of the early French winter colors, the elegant pin striped suit her father wore, still
buttoned as he lay on his back, blood dripping down his
cheeks and neck from the bullet entries. A premonition
frightened her that the call had to do with her nightmare
memory.

She reached to the receiver willing away long dead
voices, her uncle and father discussing bribes to the local
prefecture, perhaps allowing enough time to avoid the first
of the roundups and find a way to Marseilles, to escape. By
the end of 1943 the Nazis had deported 59,000 of the 350,000
Jews in France, including Rebecca Epstein's mother and little
sister, in sealed railway cars.

"Becky, it's Philippe. How are you?"

"I just walked in the house. How long has it been Phil?
Two years? Fine. We're all fine. And you?"

"The retail book business is good. We opened our third
store. Columbus Avenue. My oldest graduates from dental

school this year. Thank God the Vietnam War ended. Both boys are eligible for the draft."

"So when did you start thanking God Philippe?"

"How are yours?"

"Ami at N.Y.U. Theater. She lives there. In the dorm. Harvey is getting engaged. We like her. He got his MBA. He's thinking about law school. And Mel is still working long hours. Being on Seventh Avenue I've got a full closet of the latest from Women's Wear Daily."

She knew family catch up was sincere, but preliminary. His next words explained her traversing back 36 years on that first ring.

"I saw him, Becky. Coming up the subway stairs at East 86th Street. Keitel. I followed him. He's heavier. Stooped. Still with short hair. Grey. He entered a restaurant. Old Heidelberg it's called."

She was back there again. He was a propaganda poster for the SS. Strong jaw. Blond hair cropped to the skin. The officer's uniform was tailored around six feet of Teutonic hardness. Black boots reflecting light like a showroom Mercedes. After killing her father he removed a silver cigarette case from an inside pocket and lit up. Since being stationed in France he favored Gauloises. A slow pleasurable inhale as he gestured at the soldiers to put the troublemaker lawyer's body in the truck. They would deprive the family of a funeral.

"I waited a few minutes and went in but he wasn't there. I stood at the bar and then there he was in the mirror. In a waiter's uniform. Major Kurt Keitel. A fat old man waiting tables in Yorkville."

She leaned against the kitchen counter and said, "Oh my God Phil."

"So now there's a God?"

"What should we do?"

"We should meet."

"I'm in the city tomorrow evening for a fashion showing, dinner, a business function at Mel's company. I'll come in early."

"Meet me at the store. The one in the Village."

Rebecca went back out to the driveway where she'd left the door to the Cadillac open and got her second bag of groceries. Seeing the Skippy Peanut Butter, the Swanson Frozen Dinners, familiar American brands, anchored her back to the present, to 1976; to what was now her life. When the Germans marched into Paris she was in her third year at the Sorbonne studying biology with plans to attend medical school but the war interrupted her education and like millions of others, the course of her life. The Epstein males had been lawyers for generations and her father's clients were some of the major wine producers in Burgundy. They had an apartment in the 16th arrondisement and a small estate and vineyard in St. Thibault. They were above all French without thinking about it, and their close friends were the rural families involved in the business of grapes.

One of those families, the Miaihles, took her in as one of their own. The Germans showed an interest in her only as a beautiful young French woman, never suspecting her origins. When the Armee Juive was founded in Toulouse in 1942 she was recruited and used in missions with low odds for survival. At the end of the war and back in Paris without any family left, Master Sergeant Mel Cohen entered her life. They were married in Brooklyn in 1947 at the Flatbush Jewish Center and lived with his parents while she completed her degree at Hunter College and he got a job as an accountant at a ladies fashion manufacturer. Mel was now Executive Vice President and Chief Financial Officer at one of the hottest design firms on Seventh Avenue and Rebecca was an Associate Professor of Psychology at Queens College. Her co-workers and the ladies of Great Neck found her whiff of a French accent and stylish presence put her in a category separate from their own ordinariness. Not that many of them weren't equally stylish, but peeking through her carriage and gentleness were experiences some determined as very different from their own.

The book store on 8th Street in Greenwich Village was a large crowded brightly lit success story. Philippe Strauss's family owned a respected publishing house in France before the war and although the Germans stole all their assets putting them out of business they had relationships in New York that financed their first retail endeavor, which was on its way to becoming a chain. There was a Friday night Greenwich Village buzz as Rebecca merged with shoppers browsing and buying. She spotted Philippe on the balcony level and as she walked up the stairs thought he was as lean and lanky as when they'd met 35 years before in Toulouse.

"Becky, it's been too long," and a quick embrace that anybody who noticed could tell they had known life's tragedies together.

"There's a conference room back here we can use. You look wonderful."

"Dinner at Lutece in an hour with some big customers of Mel's from England. They own department stores. It's always a nice change from academia. Philippe. You have no doubt it's him?"

"No. No doubt. It's Keitel. He wouldn't fit in his uniform, but he still has that smug swagger. When I followed him on 86th Street it all came back. All of it like it was still happening. I wanted to kill him."

"We almost did Philippe. In the brothel. We got the captain and the other major. One of the girls too. She was a mistake. But he got away. It would have been okay then. But now?"

"We made a vow we would get him. Even if it was after the war. Of course you're right. In '43 we were fighting evil. Now it would be murder."

The conference room was near the rest rooms and a mother with a little girl went by. Rebecca saw her sister who died at Auschwitz.

"Philippe. Are we sitting here discussing whether or not we should kill Keitel? We have children in college. We are now Americans. We've lived longer here than we did in

France. You have a wife. I have a husband. We once did what we had to. We survived. A miracle. We have good lives."

"You witnessed him murder your father. He was in charge of the round ups. How many thousands was he responsible for?

"We could alert immigration. He's a Nazi war criminal. Crimes against humanity. There's a process. This conversation is madness."

"Vestigial madness."

"Philippe the philosopher. The analyst. It was the Germans who were mad. We responded. We did what we had to."

"Becky. We tried to kill him twice. After the whore house we thought we had him in Paris, leaving Tour D' Argent. Remember? They were talking about how delicious the duck was. Remember July? During the first roundup? Remember Becky? They kept 4000 Jewish children in the Velodrome d'Hiver for 5 days. No food. No Water. Filth. Then to Drancy. Were they ever heard from again Becky? But the duck was succulent."

She dissolved deep in the chair. Lighting in the small conference room was harsh. In less than an hour she'd be in one of New York's great French restaurants with famous designers and international trend setters, making her husband proud. These evenings in the city were refreshment. At age fifty-five, men still flirted, especially the Europeans, on summer Sunday afternoons in their ascots and Italian shoes at Easthampton.

"Murder is murder Philippe. We'd be found out. Trials. Going from the courthouse to the car with a newspaper over your face. Reporters. Flashbulbs. Imagine the news reports. Prison. Think of Irene. Your children. My children."

"Yes the children. We watched them leave Drancy for Auschwitz. Little ones holding hands. Remember Keitel standing there? His pale blue eyes and the cigarette. His expression. Performing necessary work for the Fatherland."

"I'm not questioning whether Keitel deserves to die. It's the risk. We beat the odds and survived. We're civilized humanity. It's maniacal to by choice take that risk. We'd become them."

"When we sabotaged and ambushed we weren't choir boys. This is merely a continuation. Unfinished business."

"It's merely murder. What's wrong with alerting the authorities? Some agency. There's a process."

"Nothing's wrong. What you say is correct. But for this Becky. Seeing him on 86th Street blending in, thinking he got away with it, I haven't slept, the SS insignia on his uniform keeps appearing in my dreams, I wake up in the night, Irene asked what's on my mind. What's on my mind is that I have this fantasy of confronting him, asking if he knows who I am, who you are, reminding him, of your father, the children, seeing his expression, and then watching him die in agony. I haven't yet determined how."

The mother and child returned from the rest room and the little girl smiled at Rebecca.

"I've got to be up town in twenty minutes Philippe. I'm worried about you."

They both got up. "Come to Old Heidelberg with me. I want you to see him."

"No."

"He's so close Becky. Don't you see? We are presented with another chance."

"Another chance for what? To go back? Vengeance? We should call some government immigration agency. They have a department that handles things like this."

"Do you recall what we vowed when Keitel and the other SS officers were leaving Tour D' Argent and there were too many of them?"

"I remember."

"Say it Becky."

"We were different people then."

"Please. Say it."

"It was something like, if one of us lives we promise the other Keitel will not be so lucky a third time. Something like that."

"We said if one of us is killed the other will not rest till Keitel is accounted for. Dead. That was our promise. Then we separated into the crowd. We didn't meet again for a month, when you came back from Switzerland with the money."

"I remember."

"Think about it Becky. Come to Old Heidelberg with me. Have a look at him. And then decide."

"Is the store always this busy?"

"It's Friday night. Weekends in the Village are good. I'm going to call you on Monday."

He walked out onto 8th Street with her as a cab was letting a passenger out. Their usual quick hug lasted longer than both expected. He stood there watching the taxi disappear into traffic.

The taxi was a clean one, owner operated, Myron Hymonowitz, with an air freshener on the dashboard. Twenty minutes to travel from German occupied France to the latest issue of Vogue. Philippe hadn't lost any relations. Comrades yes. Family no. She lost everyone. He had a gentleness but the revenge gene was firing with hotness. Keitel in Manhattan, minutes away. The one she was a resistance fighter with and loved as only warrior's love regressed to a time when savagery was good and necessary, and an evening she planned to enjoy now tilted by ghosts from the beyond. Try to disassociate. Be the wife Mel adores. Charming. Reserved. The wise sparkle. The barest flavor of pricey perfume. As the doorman in front of Lutece welcomed her with a smile and a slight bow a paralyzing moment. Why wouldn't I want to kill Keitel?

The Brits were charming, at first a bit reserved, but all twinkly after the second martini, he in Dunhill, she in Dior. Her great grandfather founded the pricey chain and her husband, now a Director, felt he'd made his niche in the fashion end of retail, especially the rather expensive coterie department. He never got enough of Seventh Avenue or the Paris shows, and was suspected of sharing a bed with the odd runway model, or for occasional spiciness the hottest male designer, if fashionably angular enough. They both immediately fell in love with Rebecca, especially her riffs of French accent. Mel's partner's wife Harriet gave Rebecca an air kiss and whispered, "these two are a trip and a half." Harriet showed an excess twenty five pounds without rancor. Mel's partner Herbie stood up and gave Rebecca kisses on each cheek continental style, which amused, and did lighten her mood.

Rebecca ordered a Kir and prayed nobody noticed half of it went down too quickly. She was seated next to the department store heiress whose chatty sing songy British lilt reminded Rebecca of a younger Julia Childs. "I looove New York," she said, "except this time of year I'll be missing two weeks of hunting. We have a place in the Haythrop country near Chipping Norton."

Dunhill smiled at Dior revealing crooked teeth. "Lavinia goes dotty if her legs aren't wrapped around a horse 3 days a week. I fell in love with a country girl. The original Sloan Ranger. One gets used to sharing the sheets with two labs and a Jack Russell." He blew her a kiss. She puckered her lips in response. Harriet said, "What a wonderful picture for a Christmas card. The five of you in bed with Reginald wearing a Santa hat. I hope you send us one."

"Oooh that's brilliant. Simply brilliant," said Lavinia. "We must do it Reginald."

Rebecca finished the Kir in quick but ladylike sips and Mel noticed her eye-signal the waiter for another.

Reginald now spoke to Harriet and Rebecca. "New York ladies are so elegant. If I didn't select Lavinia's clothes she'd show up in riding britches, Wellies and a Barbour jacket."

"And mummy's pearls," said Lavinia. More blowing kisses and lip puckering.

"Where are you staying?" asked Rebecca.

"We're at the Carlyle. I adore walking around the neighborhoods when Reginald's in meetings. In fact today I wandered up to that German part of town, Yorkville I think you call it. We love the ethnic restaurants. In London it's either Pakistani or Indian. New York is a treasure trove of ethnicity. I went by one called Old Heidelberg this afternoon. There's hardly any German restaurants in London. Memories of the blitz I suppose. We're thinking of dinner there Saturday evening. It would be lovely if you could join us."

"Haven't been there in years," said Herbert Wasserman. I believe they have oompah music on weekends." Then turning to Harriet, "Reginald and his buyers will be back in the showroom all afternoon tomorrow looking at the line. Game for some schnitzel tomorrow night dear?"

Harriet did her part for the company when called upon. "Only if we get a table far from the tuba Herbie. And if Becky and Mel come to the party."

"It's settled then," said Reginald. "And now I'm ravenous. I noticed they have duck on the menu. My favorite. Shall we order?"

The drives back to Great Neck after entertaining in Manhattan usually went quickly as Mel and Rebecca hashed over the highlights. They'd been married thirty years and Mel was as much in love with the now fifty-six year old college professor and mother of their children as with the gaunt twenty-four year old French Jewish partisan he'd met in Paris on August 25, 1944. Although the evening was filled with amusing moments her expression reminded him of those first days when she was vulnerable and hungry and he was a lean combat sergeant liberating the city. Gunfire from Parisians seeking revenge against Germans was intermittent, but could be deadly and as he and some buddies ducked into a doorway one of them said "Jesus Christ Cohen, we can still get our asses shot off," and when the shooting stopped a French girl who Mel saw needed about 15 pounds for the beauty that was there to define itself said to him, "Did I hear them call you Cohen?"

"You did. Mel Cohen. Brooklyn. New York. U.S.A."

"Thank you Mel Cohen We've been waiting 4 years. Welcome to Paris. I am Rebecca Epstein."

"Epstein and Cohen. Sounds like an accounting firm."

"I understand," and she kissed him on both cheeks.

On their first wedding anniversary he'd said life began at that moment.

They drove over the Triboro Bridge in late Friday night traffic when he finally found the words that might bring her out.

"What'd you think of the D and D duo?"

She smiled. "Dunhill and Dior?"

"He and his buyers were crazy about the preview we gave them today. Be great for the business to have a presence in England."

"I know I was off tonight."

"Maybe a little subdued, but D and D were charmed. Think you can take another night with them? Two in a row is asking a lot, but they are zany enough to be entertaining."

She envisioned the group in high spirits being served platters of red cabbage and wurst by the man she witnessed murder her father, then recalled a scene in front of the Gestapo building at Rue des Saussaies, a woman she knew had been helpful being escorted through the entrance by two plainclothes Nazis. The woman looked like those dead hare the peasants shot during hunting season.

"Would it be awful if I begged off Mel?"

"Of course not. We'll think of something."

At 11:30 Saturday morning Rebecca was out the door with the car keys in her hand late for yoga when the phone rang. She hesitated and went back in.

"Becky, it's Harriet. Herbie just called to say Mel tells him you're leaving us stranded tonight with the Duke and Duchess of Windsor. I'm not opposed to bribery. Kidnapping. Blackmail. It will be torture without you Becky. Please

please please. They're really not that bad. Aren't you dying to hear Lady Poopsie tell us about hunting, shmunting, in the Be Bop country near Chipping Pipick?"

"Harriet, I'm laughing, and I haven't in a couple of days."

"So come already. We'll laugh together."

"I can't. Really. Something's come up. It's personal. Please understand. Someday maybe we'll talk."

"Can I do anything?"

"Nothing. If you could I'd tell you. I'm sorry."

"I'm here for you Becky. We love you."

The noon yoga class on Saturdays at the Great Neck Harmony Spa was led by an 80 year old off white high pitched Indian vegetarian who the ladies said weighed 20 pounds more than his age. It was one hour of the weekend Rebecca would schedule around. She enjoyed the stretching, the 10 minutes of meditation on the mat that ended the session, and going for herbal tea with some of the ladies afterward. Turning Harriet down was painful and she tried escaping into each position. Zone out time was anything but. Mel and Harriet and Herbie were understanding but she reviled disappointing them. Go back to Deutschland and die Keitel. Please. Just die. It's all come back. I confess on my yoga mat. I want you to die.

In the tea shop their conversation bypassed her and the ladies missed her usual notes of irony. When the party ended she went to the pay phone instead of leaving with the group.

"Mel. It's Becky. I've decided to come tonight."

"That's wonderful. The Brits just bought the entire line. Huge promotion budget. Could be the biggest order we ever placed. England swings like a pendulum do. Beatles? And it never came up that you begged off tonight. We have lots to celebrate."

"I'll take the train and meet you at the office. We can arrive at Old Heidelberg together."

"I'll have a limo. 6:30 okay?

Driving to the station and then waiting on the platform something was gathering in her, a roiling dread at seeing him, the high fear and focus on mission, activated back from long dormancy. She wanted something from Keitel and now forgave Philippe. Walking the three blocks up 7th Avenue from Penn Station her pace became unladylike and she checked it. Even though it was Saturday evening the office and showroom still had several employees, and Becky saw that they were jubilant. Dom Perignon and paper cups were remnants of the celebration. The lingering designers and skeletal showroom models and all year tanned salesmen wanted the triumph to last. They hugged Becky and the smiles and kisses reminded her for them the evening had nothing to do with Nazis or the Resistance or old vows. She wanted to tell Mel about Keitel but Herbie and Harriet were at the other end of the showroom waving and they'd all be in the limo together and she and Mel wouldn't have a moment alone till their drive home. A jolt of shame at not bringing it up sooner, and then Harriet overwhelming with her genuine gratefulness and size 14 billowing chicness.

The Fugazy Limosine was idling right in front of the building with Guido their usual driver leaning against it smoking a Marlboro. Seeing the foursome enter the revolving door he stamped out the cigarette and opened the door of the big Lincoln greeting Mel and Herbie with a little more familiarity than he'd show the bankers or Wall Street types who were also his regulars.

Guido professionally maneuvered the big limo across town through heavy stop and go traffic. Herbie had taken a Styrofoam cup of Dom Perignon, offered a toasting motion and drained it. "Word must be out about the Brits big order cause we got a call from Bloomies. Their buyers are coming in on Monday. Nothing like a big hit to work up an appetite. Think we can get some Dom P at Old Heidelberg?"

"You might have to settle for Liebfraumilch Herbie," said Harriet.

Traffic was moving quicker up Third Avenue and as they got closer to 86th Street Rebecca was feeling a loneliness constriction. She was with people who cared for her in the safety of this moving leather and black luster symbol of security, but the SS were looking for her. The children of Drancy were being loaded on the trains to Auschwitz. She was learning how to shoot one of the Sten guns the British had parachuted in. Keitel was pointing his pistol at her father's head.

Guido double parked in front of Old Heidelberg and moved quickly to open the curb side door. Traffic sounds and fumes as passersby observed two well heeled couples about to have a Saturday night in Germantown. The maitre d' was balding with a grey fringe in a well used tuxedo and wire rimmed glasses. A solicitous bow saying, "The other couple is already at your table Mr. Cohen," and they followed him in to the large wood paneled dining room. Big blue and white ceramic beer steins on shelves and blow ups of Heidelberg and the Bavarian Alps on the walls. Kisses and squeals from Lavinia and Reginald.

"We're tickled to death our happy little group could have a repeat. This has been such a marvy trip for us," said Lavinia. We're flying home tomorrow, so this is our bon voyage dinner."

"And a celebration," said Reggie. "The line will be a sensation when it hits our stores. I've phoned our marketing people and they're already thinking about a major blitz. Full-page newspaper advertising, TV, P.R. You all must come to London when the promotion blasts off. I simply love your interpretation of the classic A-line skirt. It's pure design genius to create something new out of a classic. We must have some champagne."

"I like the way you Brits think," said Herbie. "Dom P if they have it."

"Our waiter is a dear," said Lavinia. "He's the sweetest roley poley cherub from cuckoo clock land. What did he say his name was Reggie? Have him bring us the bubbly."

"Yes my bubbly queen," said Reggie. "Didn't he say his name was Rudolf?"

So Major Kurt Keitel is now Rudolf, thought Becky. The Nazi that shot father in the back of the head as mama and my sister witnessed it is about to appear and serve us dinner. Can I eat from the plates he will touch, appear as if this is a special evening with these dizzy Brits, not convulse or vomit? It's just another operation Becky. Back when. You're safe now. No possibility of arrest and torture and isolation in a small dank concrete space. I've never until now understood the phrase, I need a drink. With a small smile must control my hands from trembling. What a comfort everybody is so gabby. A few deep yoga breaths Becky. Subtle.

"Ooh there he is Reggie," said Lavinia. "Rudolf. Wave him over dearest."

Reginald in his blazer and striped shirt with polka dot ascot raised both hands in an animated gesture, gold fox head cuff links showing as his jacket sleeves went half way up his arms.

"A little too much cuff showing sweetie," said Lavinia, poking him with an elbow at her witticism.

Major Kurt Keitel was at the other end of the room clearing a table and responded with an obsequious smile and enthusiastic head shaking. The deep breaths had surprisingly calmed Rebecca as she observed the now pear shaped former SS officer approach, vestiges of an imperious strut combating a humble waddle. His pale blue eyes once scheming and mean now watery.

"How may I please you sir"?

His voice was a high pitched comically accented squeak. Effeminate thought Becky. A German Truman Capote struggling with English. Then the realization that she'd never heard Major Kurt Keitel speak.

"We'd like to order some champagne, my good man Rudolf. Dom Perignon if possible," said Reggie.

He looked to the heavens as if begging for leniency and said, "Dom Perignon." He shook his head no conveying great pain. "May I suggest another French wine, Dopf-Cremant d'Asace. Very special. I think you like."

"An excellent choice my good man Rudolf," said Herbie. "Perhaps two bottles."

Keitel bowed and clicked his heels in an about face.

"Herbie never heard of Dopf Cremate," said Harriet. "I think he's tipsy."

"It's Dopf-Cremant," said Herbie. "And I am tipsy."

"How marvelous," said Reginald.

Cremate is a bad choice of word for me right now, thought Rebecca.

"You two seem so perfectly matched Lavinia. How did you and Reggie meet?" asked Harriet.

"Oh goody. We can all tell how we met. I was hunting with the Quorn. We'd been going hard most of the day and came to a big hedge. I was on a borrowed horse who was performing brilliantly, jumping like a deer, and Reggie, who I'd spotted earlier in the day for being turned out flawlessly but riding recklessly, a menace really, the sort you simply avoid when hounds are running, well Reggie approached the hedge at an angle and brushed against my horse in mid-air and we both came a cropper. Miracle we didn't break anything. I held onto my reins but Reggie's horse galloped on with the field. He was so mortified, so apologetic, like a little boy actually, stammering and blithering it was his fault and mortifying and on and on like that. He was sooo cute. I told him to give me a leg up and I'd catch his horse. When he touched my leg I felt electricity. All tingly. Oh my, I thought. Took forever, but when I caught up his mount was standing at a big gate in a boggy area all lathered up with the reins hanging down. I trotted up to him and he seemed almost grateful to be caught. Hounds and the field were nowhere to be seen or heard. I back tracked for what seemed like miles not knowing the country and when I almost decided to give up and look for a road I saw this forlorn creature on the other side of a trappy swale waving his hat and although he was to far to hear I could tell he was screaming like a banshee. Don't know what a banshee is but he was screaming like one. I trotted toward him, perhaps a quarter of a mile. When I reached him he said, "If you're not already taken I think I'd like to marry you. And two years later we did."

"What were you thinking when you saw her ride off?" asked Mel.

Reggie said, "Well there I was sitting in the mud a bit dazed and feeling very foolish and alone in the quiet countryside with nothing but the sound of crows in the middle distance. Very solitary, wondering who this ravishing woman was with the marvelous derriere I couldn't help noticing as I helped her back in the saddle. Although a bit wobbly I started walking in the direction she'd galloped off in. It was a wet day and trudging through boggy terrain in riding boots weighted down in mud is no picnic. Eventually about half a mile away silhouetted against the sky was a lone rider leading a horse. I knew it was her, and thought I'd propose at the earliest opportunity."

Keitel appeared with an ice bucket and two bottles of champagne.

"Ah Rudolf, my good man," said Herbie.

"Ah Herbie, my good man," said Harriet.

With exaggerated ceremonial flourishes Keitel inspected each champagne flute and placed one in front of each of them. Rebecca had to put both hands on the table to steady herself as he leaned over. Mel saw her face lose color and was going to say something when Lavinia blurted out, "A chance encounter while foxhunting and two lives changed for all eternity. Now Harriet, your turn. Tell us about your chance encounter with Herbert. Isn't that how it all seems to work? Chance encounters, electricity, and then you're at the altar."

"We didn't have any foxes on Ocean Parkway in Brooklyn, except occasionally a fox stole wrapped around an aunt's shoulders. Herbie, remember how we met?"

Herbie was focused on Keitel pouring the champagne.

"Of course I do. I was still in uniform. On crutches."

Harriet laughed. "The war had ended and the men were coming home. Herbie hadn't yet been discharged and was stationed at Fort Dix."

"War injury?" asked Reggie.

Harriet laughed again. "Tell Reggie how you got your war injury, my hero."

"I was in the Battalion headquarters office and a Royal typewriter fell on my foot. Smashed my big toe and two others. Hurt like hell. Schlepped around on those crutches for six weeks."

"He looked very dashing in his lieutenant's uniform," said Harriet.

"I did have a good conduct medal on my chest."

"Jolly good," said Reggie, impatient for Keitel to get to him.

"Out with it," said Lavania. "The first electrical jolt."

"It took a while to get to full charge," said Harriet.

"Not me," said Herbie. "I was giving off hot sparks immediately. It was at my cousin Roz's wedding. We were both at the singles table."

"Singles table?" said Reggie and Lavinia in unison.

"At big weddings in Brooklyn, Queens, the Bronx it's a tradition to put the unattached relatives and friends at the same table. Emotions are running at peak levels. It's a wedding. Astonishing how many couplings result."

"Singles table," they both repeated, reflecting on it.

"And just like you Reggie, I couldn't stop focusing on her derriere."

"I thought it was my boobs dahling," said Harriet.

"A couple of days later I got her number from Roz's mother, my aunt, and asked her out. She said she was busy. Took persistence. Three phone calls. Three days in a row."

"Even though the war was over I thought it was my patriotic duty to have one date with this soldier on crutches."

"We went to the movies," said Herbie.

Lavinia watched Keitel pouring and after a moment said, "I bet you remember the film."

"What was the film Herbie?" said Harriet.

"Throw me a tough one baby. It was The Best Years of our Lives with Fredrick March."

"We both cried," said Harriet.

"Lovely," said Lavinia.

Keitel had filled all six glasses and with an overt show of discretion stepped back awaiting approval.

Reginald raised his flute and studied the tiny bubbles doing their dance. He cleared his throat, had all eyes, and after a theatrical pause said, "When business friends become true friends it is cause for jubilation. To our new true friends, and to a celebration of ingenious fashion design. Let us drink." The group offered a toasting gesture and savored the champagne. Reginald nodded affirmation at Keitel who bowed looking very pleased and shuffled off.

"That was charming Reggie," said Lavinia. "He's so clever with words. And now we must hear from Mel and Rebecca. When was your moment?"

Rebecca watched Keitel's bulky figure disappear through the swinging doors into the kitchen and the contents of her glass went down as if in slow motion. Mel saw she was the only one with an empty flute.

Herbie said, "Mel is the actual war hero. Landed on the beaches of Normandy, fought across France, liberated Paris, the Battle of the Bulge, Bronze Stars with Oak Leaf Cluster, Purple Hearts. He found his beautiful bride in Paris on liberation day."

While Lavinia chattered on about this one sounding like a movie Mel put his arm around Becky's chair and without moving his lips leaned in and whispered, "You're not well. What's going on?"

Becky murmured, "On the way home."

Lavinia said, "Okay Becky, since we're now true friends may I call you Becky? You're it. Or will Mel begin the saga? And don't leave out that first moment of electrical currents."

He gave her shoulder a soft reassuring squeeze as Reggie said, "I was also invited to the D-Day party. Where did you come ashore Mel?"

"Omaha."

Reggie said, "Gold. Fiftieth Northumbrian. We landed on the Ver sur Mer side of the beach. Pretty nasty. Of course nobody had a rougher time than you yanks on Omaha."

Mel hesitated, his arm still around Becky's chair. "The beach was heavy going. Steep terrain. German fire never stopped. My unit eventually met up with your Royal Marines in the area around Port-en-Bessin."

"That night we linked up with some Canadians from Juno," said Reggie. "Forget the name of the town."

"It was over thirty years ago. We've both forgot a lot," said Mel. "Probably a good thing."

Reggie fingered his champagne glass, not being there for the moment, then got up and gave Mel an embrace, saying louder than he realized, "Bloody fucking Krauts."

Four musicians dressed in lederhosen were setting up on the other side of the room.

"Okay boys. Let's segue from war to love," said Harriet. "We only know bits of the full story about France, Paris, how you two met. Becky?"

Rebecca gestured at her empty glass and Harriet reached over to the champagne bucket and filled both of theirs, then passed it around. Keitel appeared like a gnome bursting from under a frond in the forest and officiously took over, emptying the first bottle and uncorking the second.

Overhearing Reggie curse the Germans reignited enough partisan vestige buried in Becky that the vulnerability dissipated. She looked to Mel and again uncharacteristically drank down half the champagne. Her look was languid, and Mel felt a flash back to her eyes the first time they did it. She smiled more to Mel than the group. There was stillness at their table that sometimes occurs in meetings when everybody is focusing hard to truly understand what is being said.

Harriet prompted her. "It was Paris on liberation day, wasn't it?"

"Yes. Liberation. But the word isn't strong enough. De-Gaule returned. The Americans marching in formation.

Endless lines. We loved them all. Every one of them. At last it was over. There was still shooting. Our people seeking revenge. And the Germans firing back. Isolated. But bystanders could be hit. Some were killed. Over. Yet some were killed. I was back in Paris. Searching for Philippe. Philippe Blime. My friend. He's here now. We see them sometimes. Our families. Shots were very close. Very loud. People scrambled for shelter. I ran for a doorway with some American soldiers. Mel was one of them. He introduced himself. Said his name was Cohen. From Brooklyn. They were still shooting. Single shots and then a machine gun. I kissed him on both cheeks and told him my name was Epstein. And he said Epstein and Cohen. Sounds like an accounting firm. He was making a joke. I hadn't heard jokes like that in very long. Then the shooting stopped. I can't say it was electricity Lavinia, but it was safety and relief and connection, deep human connection from thousands of years. I think it was something more enduring than electricity. He said I was too skinny and looked in his pack for food. It was Spam and crackers and two small cans of peaches. I was embarrassed. He made me take them and then his men shouted for him to catch up with his unit. He said they were staying in Paris for a while, he couldn't say how long, and wanted to feed me. That's what he said. He wanted to feed me. I didn't know what state our family apartment was in. Who might be living there. My father was dead and mother and sister had been sent to Auschwitz and were probably dead. The only address I could think of was the last safe house. He wrote it down and said, 'I'll find you Epstein', then ran to catch up with his men. Later I found Philippe at that safe house. There were a few others from the Armee Juive. We could stay a while. Weeks. Even months. A waiter in the café across the street told us the owner had been arrested by the Gestapo a month before and most probably tortured to death. Even though the Germans knew it was over they couldn't stop. But it was over. For more than three years we didn't think beyond the next operation. The next day even. Although Philippe's family had all their assets confiscated by the Nazis they were alive. I had no one. But I could plan my tomorrows. I was twenty four, a free French citizen, find a way to return to university, get a job, grateful to be living. But no family. No one. How to begin? The following days there were long walks. Strolled around the Sorbonne. Walked by our building in the sixteenth arrondisement. It hadn't changed. Except everything changed. I kept walking too numb to let the anguish become a sob. That came later. Back at the safe house, what had been a safe house, one of the others said an American sergeant had been by asking for me. He left a note. Mel asked if we could meet the next evening. His handwriting was so neat. Precise little letters. Not like 'I'm Cohen from Brooklyn' and 'Epstein and Cohen sounds like an accounting firm.' I didn't know how to reach him but I made sure I was at the house the next evening. He showed up at 7pm in a different uniform. With a tie. No rifle. A bag with fruit and bread and meat. Food was still scarce and there was enough for the others. We walked. The streets were still crowded with Parisians celebrating. There was a café on a side street. We talked. And ate," then looking at Mel, "and gradually electricity." Keitel appeared with very large menus.

"After that we saw each other whenever Mel could get away. He would always bring groceries. The others in the house encouraged the relationship. Food after all," Mel said, "It needed no encouragement. We still had Germany to deal with and I knew my time in Paris was going to end. When it did we were committed."

"What happened next?" asked Reggie.

"More fighting. Battle of the Bulge. Germany. Berlin. Whenever we had a mail call there was a letter from Becky. After the Germans surrendered I managed a week back in Paris. Then back to Germany. Then discharged. Lots of red tape and eventually got Becky to New York. And here we are."

"How beautiful," said Lavinia.

"There are countless stories like ours," said Becky. "American soldiers and French girls falling in love. American boys with British girls", Lavinia nodded, "German girls, it's a story as old as armies occupying distant lands. Even French girls and German soldiers during the occupation. But it didn't end well for them. Those girls had their heads shaved. Swastikas painted on their faces. Shunned. Because they fell in love with the enemy."

"Not all German soldiers were believers. Nazis," said Mel. "And the girls were naïve. Or hungry. Some could have been sympathizers. Or just stupid. They got what they deserved."

He watched Becky drink down the rest of her champagne in one gulp and look to the beaded green bottle in the ice bucket.

"To keep hating them it has to be personal," said Reggie. "Having chums shot and watching them die. Or lose a limb. Or a relative in the blitz. The way my mother and grandmother died in London when a V2 rocket demolished their building. Has to be personal. And even then time seems to take the edge off. Here we are in a German restaurant about to dine on Kraut food served by a waiter who was probably in the Werhmacht, while being serenaded by oompah music. It really is mad isn't it?"

Herbie added, "And many of the cabs in Israel are Mercedes Benzes."

Lavinia said, "Do you really think Rudolf was in the German army? Let's ask him what he did in the war."

"I'm not sure that's a good idea," said Reggie.

Lavinia showed an involuntary pout, as one accustomed to having things go as she would like, then brightened. "Don't be silly sweetie. He's such an agreeable little elf. Or not so little elf," she said with a girlish giggle. "I'll do it."

Reggie shrugged and looked heavenward, a gesture the others saw was part of their repertoire.

"Some more champagne please," said Becky.

Reggie passed the bottle across the table to Mel. He hesitated, then poured, feeling a gathering unease with Becky, always impeccable in social situations. The former combat soldier recognized a be alert signal.

Keitel once again was there, a presence appearing without warning, pad poised. He said the duck and the whole fish were specials and took their orders, nodding with great approval as each made their selections. Inspecting the almost empty champagne bottle he said, "May I bring another?"

Before anyone could respond Mel waved him away with, "I think we've had enough for the time being."

Keitel offered an obedient bow and as he turned Lavinia said, "Rudolf, our drinks conversation was getting philosophical, what a crazy world we live in, that sort of thing, and since you are obviously a man of great manners I wondered if I could ask a question of a personal nature?"

"Of course madam. It would be my honor."

"Not bad," Reggie exhaled, looking to Mel.

"Well," Lavinia reflected, "the subject of the war came up, each of us describing where they were, and I was wondering what a man of your charm might have been doing during those years. A general's aide perhaps?"

A gay laugh, showing enjoyment at this personal interest in their waiter. "The lady flatters me. I was a lowly cook. A private. At a training base outside of Nuremberg. I was lucky. Spent the whole war peeling potatoes. Ha ha."

"The whole war in Nuremberg Major? Peeling potatoes?" said Rebecca.

"Ya. Nuremberg. Thank you. I put your order in now."

He shuffled toward the kitchen at a restrained quickened clip.

The first notes of the tuba and accordion filled the room with Valderie, Valderah, Oh may I go a wandering, set to a polka beat.

Lavinia swayed to the music. "This is such fun. See what we learned? Rudolf was peeling potatoes. Not shooting at us. Did I hear you call our private a major Becky? Seemed a bit nervous at his promotion."

"Just came out like that. He is our majordomo."

The music segued to a medley from The Student Prince and the conversation was now about the fashion scene in

London and then the Paris shows. About thirty minutes passed as a female singer made up to look like Marlene Dietrich with twenty excess pounds wrapped in sequins sang Lily Marlene with much emotion and just when Herbie yawned he was getting hungry a large breasted waitress with a single long blond braid appeared carrying their first course.

"What's happened to Rudolf the Remarkable. A charmer he is," said Reggie.

"A sudden stomach virus. He couldn't continue. Asked to be excused. Sends his apologies. I'll be your server. I'm Brunhilda. Call me Hildy."

Appetizers didn't last long, as they'd been drinking and between Keitel shuffling off and Hildy's arrival a longer than usual time elapsed, not that there were any moments without conversation. Everybody contributed, and all were equally interested in what the others had to say. By the main course Mel saw that Becky was less on edge and by the dessert crepes and coffee a pleasant cohesiveness engulfed the group. Reggie insisted on picking up the tab, his words, and they all stood in front of the restaurant embracing and saying they'd do it again in London. Herbie offered a ride in the limo back to the Carlyle but Lavania wanted to stroll through the city on their last night. More embraces and Guido delivered his regulars back to the garage on 38th Street.

Mel had WPAT on the car radio, Becky called it the Montivani station, and for a few moments they absorbed the calm of just the two of them in the Cadillac. Mel glided onto the street and flowed into the late Saturday night midtown traffic.

"They're really very nice people," said Becky. "I wouldn't mind at all meeting up with them in London."

"Imagine. Reggie and I just a couple of miles apart on the beach during D-Day. I do like them both very much."

Mel was going to wait for Becky to bring up her uncharacteristic edginess earlier in the evening as he knew she would, and it didn't take long. As they approached the Triboro Bridge she said, "Mel, there's something we should talk about. Between your hours at the office and these last couple of days with everything going on I wanted to bring this up sooner, but it just didn't happen."

He turned the radio down. They could faintly hear the strings playing Climb Every Mountain.

"This is such a coincidence but Philippe called the other day and asked if we could meet. Something important. So before going to Lutece last night I met him at the book store on 8th Street. He told me that while coming out of the subway on East 86th Street he saw somebody from the war, from our days together. I didn't want to hear, but he said it was Major Kurt Keitel, the one who killed my father. He followed him to make sure. He saw him go into a restaurant and a few minutes later Philippe went in. The restaurant was Old Heidelberg Mel, and Keitel was working there as a waiter. Rudolf. Our waiter tonight was SS Major Kurt Keitel."

Mel reached across the seat and took her hand. "How did you make it through the evening Becky?"

She shifted her body closer to him as they drove over the bridge with Manhattan's late night luminescence behind them.

"I'm so grateful to be married to you Becky."

"I don't know what to do," she said. "Philippe wants to confront him"

"We should get some legal advice. Go to Immigration. Or better yet, the Israeli Embassy."

"He wants both of us to confront him. It's complicated. We tried to get him twice. Kill him. During the occupation. But he eluded us. We made a vow. If one of us survives the war we'd complete the mission."

"You don't mean murder him."

She didn't answer. During their early years, especially when they were first married, she related some of her past in the Resistance. One summer Sunday afternoon in 1948 they had rented a rowboat in Prospect Park and as they drifted in the middle of the lake enjoying the sun and watching families with young children row by she told him about witnessing her father being murdered by an SS officer and running away, eventually joining the Armee Juive in Toulouse. She described swearing allegiance by candlelight with her hand on a pistol and getting some training at a mountain chalet in Les Michallons near St. Nizier. Another time she mentioned convincing an employee of the city of Grenoble to pilfer some forms from city hall to be forged in to false identity papers. They used her as a courier for a trip to Switzerland to pick up over fifty thousand dollars in cash which she delivered personally to Otto Ginieski, commander of the Armee Juivee. She smiled when she said his code name was Toto, which was switching the letters in Otto around. Until now it never came up that she personally attempted to assassinate anyone. The actions she was part of, and the events she witnessed, resulted in layers of resilience most women wouldn't know of. Layered in with that sort of strength was a fragility Mel acknowledged by not over talking certain subjects. There was calmness enveloping them as a couple, like an extra comforter on a cold night.

She said again, "I don't know what to do."

Eventually Mel said, "Tonight nothing."

"You know how I feel about Philippe."

"I know. It will come to you."

They turned on to Wensley Drive and their darkened house as both wished the kids were children again and home with the baby sitter.

On Sunday Mel spent a large part of the day on the phone with Herbie and some of the production people discussing details of the big British order. Becky went to a yoga session and then tried to concentrate on the classes she was to teach that week. The topic of Keitel didn't come up till evening when they went to a local Chinese restaurant for dinner.

"Chinese restaurants seem to have a tranquilizing effect," said Mel. "Wonder why that is".

"Perhaps the Wonton soup reminds you of your mother's chicken soup," said Becky.

"Then let's order the soup for two. Liquid valium with MSG and bits of pork."

"Tantalizing," she said.

"Have you had any further thoughts about Philippe? Keitel?"

"I just don't know what to do Mel. It would have been better if these old horrors were left undisturbed. What was it Lavinia said? A chance meeting and you're at the altar? A chance meeting on 86th Street and memories for the most part dormant come to life. I haven't had this feeling for revenge so strongly. It's not good Mel. I just don't know what to do."

At six thirty A.M. on Monday Mel left for the office and at nine Philippe called.

"Becky. It's Phil. I have news. I had him followed. A man who works for me, retired New York city detective, he found where he lives, East 98th Street, way over east near the brewery, in a walk up, a tenement. He changed his name to Rudolf Schmidt."

"Rudolf Schmidt? The name of the janitor at Holden Caulfield's boarding school in Catcher in the Rye. I'm sure Keitel never read it," she said. "But a coincidence over the weekend Philippe. We had dinner at Old Heidelberg on Saturday night. Some of Mel's customers from England wanted to go there. He was our waiter. It was difficult. Unbearable. When can we meet?"

"This afternoon. I'll drive out to Great Neck. Around two o'clock?"

"Fine. Two o clock. Au revoir."

She put the phone down and for a long moment realized, without meaning to, she had signed off in her first language, the language of her youth, of the resistance. She had stopped thinking in French many years before, simultaneously with becoming a U.S. citizen. The rest of the morning was filled with catching up on household things that had been neglected these last few days, laundry, vac-uuming, which she was grateful for. There was calmness in her actions, the same sort of resolve from over thirty years back when on an operation and the prospect of dying was a given, and acceptance of that possibility resulted in peace-fulness.

A little after two Philippe parked his Porsche in front of the house and walked quickly to the front door, which Re-becca opened before he could ring.

"Come in to the kitchen. Tea? Soda?"

Waving off the hospitality he sat on a counter stool and said, "You're right Becky. I was insane for days wanting to kill him. With my own hands. Strangle him. Insanity. But I must confront him. We must confront him. Had we killed him in Paris on that second attempt things would be differ-ent."

"Calling it off was the right decision," she said. "There were too many of them. And more people in the street than we planned. A fluke. It saved his life. Maybe ours."

"I don't deny that Becky. Will you come with me?"

She opened the refrigerator door and with a distracted expression looked at the Kraft American cheese and Cokes and oranges. She stood there a long time. Philippe finally said, "You're wasting Freon."

"When?" She closed the refrigerator door and sat down on the stool next to him. "Where?"

"He's off on Mondays. I told you I have his address."

"Next Monday?"

"Today is Monday Becky. Today. If we waited a week we'd go crazy. Change our minds. Today."

She shrugged and went upstairs to change while he paced around the kitchen, then went out to the car and lit up a Camel.

Philippe parked the Porsche at a garage in midtown not wanting to leave it on the street in a neighborhood without doormen and awnings. They took a taxi up to 97th and First

Avenue and walked the two blocks to the address written on memo pad paper from the book store. It was a four story walk up of railroad flats with fire escapes on each floor and an entrance that had tarnished brass mail boxes and a stale smell, a combination of cabbage cooking and disinfectant. The name Schmidt was on a buzzer marked 3 E but the building was open so they didn't ring. The wooden stairs were worn down to the grain and sounded like Keitel's squeaky voice in the shadowy light. Rebecca noticed doors to bathrooms in the hallways on each floor. A few blocks to the west were multi-million dollar co-ops.

Reaching the third floor and breathing harder they heard a toilet flush followed by a fat old woman in a ba- bushka adjusting her faded print dress emerge from the shared bathroom. Her stockings were rolled down just be- low fleshy white knees, calves showing varicose veins. She was startled to see them and her expression said I don't want involvement with you. Philippe said, "Keitel?" and she motioned to a door at the end of the dark hallway. They could hear an afternoon soap opera coming from one of the apartments. The woman wheezed down to the second floor filling most of the staircase, ignoring them.

A low wattage unfrosted light bulb hung from a frayed wire in the hallway and the linoleum runner magnified the creakiness of their footsteps. Rebecca steadied herself on Philppe's arm, surprising both of them. He rapped four taps on the door, quietly but assertively. They heard someone shuffling and Rebecca flashed Keitel's labored waitering at Old Heidelberg.

The door cracked open a few inches and the left half of former SS Major Kurt Keitel's face peered out. He saw a man in a suit who could have been an official of the government and part of a female form.

"Mister Schmidt?" said Philippe.

"Ya?"

"We'd like to talk to you."

With a look of resignation he turned away and they let themselves in. The apartment was shabby but neat with an old sofa showing wide floral slip covers, a Barca lounger with stuffing coming through a narrow slit in the green plastic seat, a frayed shag rug, a TV console on the floor with rabbit ears, a kitchen table in what was the living room with a German language newspaper and cup and saucer half full of black coffee.

He hadn't yet looked at them, sat down at the table in a gesture of surrender and said "Ya?" again.

Becky closed the door and turned the lock. The click made him look up. She moved toward him. "Remember me Major?"

Philippe checked out the bedroom and small kitchen.

Recognition and then a sense of gravity filled his rheumy eyes.

"Old Heidelberg Saturday night?"

"Further back," said Philippe.

Becky noticed several framed photographs in a glass book case. One showed a young Keitel with a woman his own age and a girl about five or six in knee socks and a short skirt taken in front of an Alpine cabin. Behind it a more recent picture of the same girl as a young woman in formal riding attire on a horse at a dressage show. Another was of Keitel and others in uniform with the Eiffel Tower as background. They each were holding a bottle of wine and had the smile of victors. Amongst the books, some in German, a ragged photo album. She picked up the framed photo and examined it for several seconds.

"Was this taken in Nuremberg where you spent the war peeling potatoes Major Keitel?"

He ignored her.

"Look at me and try to remember. Burgundy. St. Thibault. The lawyer you shot twice in the back of the head. My father. Epstein."

Keitel bent over in his chair and began rubbing his chest.

Philippe put his palm under Keitel's chin and tilted his head up.

"Think back Keitel. The Velodrome d' Hiver. Four thousand children. Five days. No food. No water. Then Drancy. Final destination Auschwitz."

"My daughter coming soon. She explain," he said in a dry screechy moan.

Rebecca went back to the book case and looked through the photo album. Pictures of SS officers including Keitel with a black German shepherd, in front of Notre Dame, the Louvre, with some laughing French girl at a cafe, in St Thibault. She gave the album to Philippe and picked up a quart size quite heavy glass beer mug with swastikas engraved on both sides. It weighed as much as lead.

"Do you remember putting my father's dead body in the truck?"

He was now mostly doubled over in the chair moaning and partly sobbing like a child with a stomach ache.

"How long after that did you deport my mother and sister?"

His gasping sounds slowed to normal breathing as he righted himself in the chair, looked at Rebecca with contempt and regaining some residue of strength coughed out "Epstein." He then said, "Yid" and spit at her face, missing, but the spit landed on her neck.

Rebecca stepped back, and then smashed Keitel in the head with the beer stein. The sound of his skull cracking and the Rorschach test of blood patterned down his cheek as if watching an abstract avant-garde art film. He crumbled in the chair and Rebecca struck again in the same spot before his body landed on the floor. A smudge of blood stained the beer mug and Keitel was in a contorted position with one cheek on the carpet. The side of his face that was visible had an open eye with no current flowing. She shifted to strike again but Philippe caught her. She then collapsed leaning her back in to him. He wrapped his arms around her. They were wedged like two large jigsaw puzzle pieces for longer than either could remember.

When Philippe thought she was steady enough to stand he found a large brown paper shopping bag in the kitchen and took the beer stein that was still in her hand, found the photo album and put them both in the bag. They stood side by side pressed in to each other staring down at the twisted grotesqueness on the frayed rug. Philippe started toward the door guiding a puppet-like Rebecca and looking around the room as if covering somebody's retreat. He made sure the door was locked and as they went down the stairs heard an Alka Seltzer commercial from the TV that had the soap opera on. "Plop plop. Fizz fizz, oh what a relief it is."

It was sunny on Ninety Eighth Street and a young woman in a tailored suit wearing running shoes and carrying a brief case smiled at them as she entered the building. She had Keitel's pale blue eyes and bone structure, wore her blond hair in a page boy, and moved with the appealing confidence that comes from being attractive, athletic, and desirable.

They got a cab on Second Avenue to the garage in midtown. Neither spoke until in Philippe's Porsche on the way back to Great Neck.

"I was going to smash his skull again. I was like them. Oh God."

Philippe said, "It took over thirty years.

She said, "To fulfill our vow."

Then she said, "Oh God. What do we do now?"

Philippe said, "Nothing."

CONTRIBUTORS' NOTES

Virginia Beards is a Seattle native who moved to Pennsylvania in 1961. A member of the original faculty of the Brandywine Campus of Penn State University, she lives on a horse farm with the expected, plus several dogs and cats.

*I did my Ph.D. dissertation on the Irish hunt writers Edith Somerville and Martin Ross whose "Irish R.M." stories and novels as well as my own ten years in a local hunt put rowel spurs to my imagination. Like them I find human, horse, and hound antics in the hunt field enormously diverting.

Jim Breslin is the author of the short story collection, *Elephant*. He is also the founder of the West Chester Story Slam. His fiction has appeared in *Think Journal*, *Metazen* and fictionaut. His nonfiction writing has appeared in *The Town Dish*, *The World According to Twitter* and the *Daily Local*. He lives in West Chester, PA, with his wife and two sons. His website is jimbreslin.com.

*Real Gentlemen was inspired by Jamie Wyeth's painting, *Lester*. I saw the portrait while at the Brandywine River Museum and found myself writing a story based on the painting. My understanding is the real Lester was Jamie Wyeth's friend. My character is obviously a fictional account.

Robb Cadigan is a Baltimore boy transplanted to Phoenixville, PA. He has worked as a forklift operator, clam shucker, mad man, and television executive, but he is happiest as a family man and a storyteller. Which are sometimes the same thing. Robb is currently at work on a novel.

*I have always liked the imagery of a road, the journeys we make, the detours we take. Chester County has some beautiful roads to walk. When I'm out there on the shoulder, I think about those who have walked these paths before, or those who may have, and where they were headed.

Wayne A. "Tony" Conaway was born in Philadelphia and still hasn't gotten over it. He graduated with a degree in Communications from West Chester University, where both his parents taught in the Music Department. Over the years, he has lived in New York, New Jersey, Georgia, and Texas, as well as Pennsylvania. He has been a professional writer since 1990, and is best known as coauthor of the best-selling *Kiss, Bow or Shake Hands?* series of business books. Also, he has twice been president of the Brandywine Valley Writers Group.

*You can't read from your business book at a bookstore signing—you'll bore people. So, for readings, I write short, amusing pieces like the two in this collection. I try to keep them short enough to read in about 7 minutes, which is the attention span of most people (it's the approximate length between television commercials).

I wrote *Fit for a King* as an assignment while taking a humor writing class from Brett Leveridge (who is a much better writer than I am, by the way). A woman in the class wrote a story about her embarrassment at going for a bra fitting; my story is a male version of that idea.

Brett Leveridge was fascinated by my reminiscences of being a big, scary youth. Apparently, scary people don't usually write comedy. *Formerly Fearsome* is a fictionalized version of my youth, but I really did inadvertently scare people when I was walking around West Chester at night.

Peter Cunniffe is a husband, father, and business professional who lives in Malvern, PA. He studied English Literature at West Chester University back in the days when New Main Hall was, well, new. Peter has just completed his first novel-length work of fiction.

*The seeds for *An Incident Near Paoli* were sown when my daughter asked me how "Battle of the Clouds Park" in

Chester County got its name. Her question inspired me to learn much of our local Revolutionary history. *An Incident Near Paoli* actually started as a children's story written as a series of letters sent home from the Revolutionary front and touting the role of Providence in keeping the cause of liberty alive. No war, no gore; just hope. Amid headlines of US soldier deaths in Iran and Afghanistan, I decided to revisit these letters. Passing one of the schools that sits on the original massacre site made we wonder how history would repeat itself (as it so often does) on that same ground.

Michael T. Dolan is the author of the novel *WALDEN*. His essays have appeared in the *Philadelphia Inquirer* and other newspapers throughout the country. He writes at www.conversari.com and lives in West Chester, PA.

*The phrase *the river runs red* jumped from my subconscious one summer evening, and along with it a visual of the final scene in this story. Both the words and the image haunted me, and I began to reflect on the darkness that sometimes lurks below the surface of our everyday lives.

Ronald D. Giles is an author, a singer, and a television executive, who has been awarded seven regional EMMYs for programs at WBZ-TV, WCPO-TV, and WBNS-TV. He was recruited to come to Chester County as part of the original management team that started QVC, where he held the positions of Executive Vice President of Broadcasting and EVP of International Electronic Retailing, having created start-up operations for QVC in Germany, Mexico, and Great Britain.

*"The Prey" is loosely based on an incident that occurred while I was turkey hunting in an Ohio state forest. I had taken my young family—daughter five, son three, and wife twenty-eight—for a weekend in a state park's "primitive cabin" section of the woods while I hunted some miles away in the early morning. The weekend was such a disaster that, among other things, Mrs. Giles thereafter defined "primitive" as a Holiday Inn and her definition hasn't changed for the last 40 years!

Terry Heyman is a former practicing attorney and fashion buyer. She has written fashion and style articles and is a frequent lecturer on intellectual property law in the fashion industry. She lives in West Chester, PA, with her husband and two children and enjoys writing fiction in her spare time.

*I'm a big fan of the Talking Head's song "Once in a Lifetime" and often think about the numerous decisions, both significant and seemingly inconsequential, which fundamentally impact the course of our lives. That was the inspiration for the character of Deborah and the events leading to her awakening. Also, years ago I lived in an apartment where the water got so hot friends claimed I could cook spaghetti in my shower.

Joan Hill lives in West Chester with her husband, their two sons, and two cairn terriers.

*In the first drafts of this story, my main character lost her way on an ordinary walk. This came from letting my mind wander while I was walking through my own neighborhood with the terriers. At first, the husband in the story was cheating with a close neighbor, but gradually, as what was most important to Matilda came into focus, I realized that the story would begin with her moving out on her own.

Jacob Asher Michael is an environmental planner from West Chester, PA. His first novel *Buddha's Thunderbolt*, won first prize at the 2006 Philadelphia Writers Conference. It was reviewed in *Science Fiction and Fantasy Magazine* by Charles DeLint, who called it, "one of the most original and entertaining reads I've had in some time." He has published short stories in *Satire*, *Barbaric Yawp* and *In the Spirit of the Buffalo*, and is the primary author of four award-winning environmental land use publications.

*The inspiration for this story was Evelyn Jordan who died of ASL in 2007. I did indeed meet her at Willow Branch Sangha, a Buddhist meeting south of West Chester, PA. Like all writers of fiction, I took a kernel of interesting truth and then added strategically placed lies to make it more dramatic. But the incident with the cloud, that really happened, and I will never forget it.

Eli Silberman is a nationally known advertising executive who spent 14 years at McCann-Erickson in New York and owned his own firm in Philadelphia for 20 years. After successfully selling the agency he spends more time on his farm in Unionville, PA, where he consults, serves on several boards, tends the farm, and writes. He has completed a novel, *E TRAIN TO MASADA*, which is currently making the rounds of agents in New York.

*While researching background material for the novel I came across a memoir of a woman who served in the underground in World War II. Further research revealed stories of the most courageous young women of the resistance who risked their lives daily in fighting evil during the German occupation of France, Poland, Ukraine, and other occupied countries. Those women were the inspiration for *The Great Neck Nazi Killer*, a short story I'm developing into a novella.

Nicole Valentine is currently obtaining her MFA in Creative Writing at the Vermont College of Fine Arts. She is the Vice President of Product/Technology for figment.com, an online writing community for young adult fiction. She lives in Chester County with her husband, daughter, and two cats. She can sometimes be found conversing with trees.

*One day I decided to follow some old signs, drive down an unassuming alley in West Goshen and find the Historical Weeping Beech. It's not easy to find it in the summer behind its thick curtain of leaves, but in the winter you can't miss it. You can't visit a three hundred year old mammoth specimen like this one, and not wonder what stories it has to tell. Those gnarled branches belied a complex history, and this story was born.

Christine Yurick is the publisher and editor of *Think Journal*. A native Chester County resident, Christine also writes poetry and is the founder of the Victory Collaborative, an annual arts event held at Victory Brewing Company. Her website is thinkjournal.com.

*This story came from my long walks on the Struble Trail, and my imagining different scenarios from the recent tragic story of Ryan Dunn's death. News reports from the crash said that Ryan and his friend, Zachary Daniel Hartwell, died in a car accident after Ryan's Porsche collided with a guardrail, landed in the woods and burst into flames. However, the story *Sam's Brother* is simply one of my imagination, that depicts the siblings of the two unfortunate friends and how they deal with grief and forgiveness.

Sue Gregson is a freelancer doing business as Inkspiration since 1996. She has nearly 30 years of experience as a writer, editor, and public relations practitioner in the public and private sectors. She is the author of more than 20 nonfiction books for children, mostly historical biographies. Her Inkspiration projects have included: editing fiction novels and short stories, including a Pushcart Prize nominee; editing and leveling more than 100 grades K-6 math books; proofreading and editing retail copy; and writing and placing marketing articles in national trade magazines. Sue lives with her family in Downingtown.

Cover Design

Larry Geiger is a graphic designer, illustrator and technologist involved in the conception, design, and production of print communications, identity programs, exhibits, environmental graphics, signage, websites, and other forms of visual communication. He helps his clients communicate ideas as a collaborator, interpreter, innovator, listener, and friend. He and his family are new transplants to the area and are proud to call Chester County "home". His website is larrygeigerdesign.com.

Photography

David James is a southern transplant from the great state of Alabama. He is a graduate of the University of Alabama in Birmingham. In his past career life he has been heard up and down the east coast on various radio stations. Seven years ago, David and his family were brought to Chester County to try a new venture in hosting for a television shopping network.

Throughout all of his many hat changes David has been taking photos for his family and friends. Recently he has started to pursue this artistic endeavor professionally. David's work can currently be seen in his living room, his mom's house and at some guys house who bought a print in Tulsa, OK. David had a blast exploring the backwoods of Chester County while shooting the cover for this book. His website is photosbydavidjames.com

ACKNOWLEDGMENT

The lyric taken from Robert Leroy Johnson's "Hell Hound On My Trail" is used with permission of Kobalt Music Publishing America on behalf of MPCA King of Spades.

CHESTER COUNTY WRITING

If you are a Chester County writer who is looking to connect with others, try the following resources.

The Brandywine Valley Writers Group meets the third Tuesday of the month. Learn more at bvwg.org.

The Main Line Writers Group meets the third Wednesday of every month. Search Main Line Writers on meetup.com.

The Philadelphia Writers Group meets the first Saturday of the month. Search Philadelphia Writers Group on meetup.com.

The West Chester Story Slam is held the second Tuesday of every month (except December.) Learn more at wcstoryslam.com.

Made in the USA
Lexington, KY
21 December 2011